UNDEAD OR ALIVE

A BAD THINGS NOVEL

New York Times and *USA Today* Bestselling Author

CYNTHIA EDEN

This book is a work of fiction. Any similarities to real people, places, or events are not intentional and are purely the result of coincidence. The characters, places, and events in this story are fictional.

Published by Cynthia Eden.

Cover art and design by: Yours Truly

Proof-reading by: J. R. T. Editing

PROLOGUE

"I need you to find someone for me."

Cassius "Cass" Garvan gave a low, rumbling laugh. "Sorry, but you'll have to get in line." He kept his legs braced apart and his hands remained loose at his sides. Maybe other paranormals would have been quaking in their boots as they stood before the big, bad Lord of the Dark...but Cass wasn't one of those lesser paranormals. And he didn't fear Luke Thorne.

Why should he?

Luke slowly turned away from the floor-to-ceiling windows that overlooked his island paradise. Paradise, prison—whatever. To Cass, it was pretty much the same thing. He'd gotten orders to show up for this little one-on-one chat with Luke, and Cass had appeared more out of curiosity than anything else.

It had been a very, very long time since Luke had spoken to him. When you were mortal—or even *immortal*—enemies with someone, you didn't call the other person up for a little casual chit-chat every day.

"You're working for my brother." Luke's face tightened when he said that one word...*brother.* As if it were a curse. Probably because to him, it was.

Cass knew the old stories about Luke and his twin brother Leo. One brother was the Lord of the Dark, the master of all the dark paranormal beings that walked—or flew—on earth. The other was the Lord of the Light, the powerhouse behind all of the so-called "good" creatures out there.

Cass didn't believe in good. Some days, he didn't believe in evil, either.

He just believed in death—death was kind of his thing.

"Leo has you chasing the fallen angel, doesn't he?" Luke stalked toward him.

Cass considered the matter for a moment. "Now that you mention it, I believe that acquiring her may be on my to-do list." He flashed a smile at Luke. "When you're the best hunter to ever live, well, let's just say that word gets around. You want someone found...you call me. I mean, sure, the shifters out there tend to have pretty good noses, but we both know they are *nothing* compared to me."

"Arrogant asshole."

"It's not arrogance if it's true." He'd never bothered much with modesty. Cass understood exactly what he was, and what he was not. "We both know I have a very particular skill set."

A muscle jerked in Luke's jaw. The Lord of the Dark was getting pissed—Cass could feel the air around them starting to heat up.

"The angel is taken care of," Luke gritted out. "And Leo will *not* be getting her back."

Cass gave a low whistle. "I hate to break it to you, but I think you're wrong. That guy is dead set on getting back his girl—"

"She isn't his."

When the angry voice spoke from behind him, Cass stiffened. Dammit. He hadn't heard the other guy approach. Cass glanced over his shoulder and saw the big, currently glaring werewolf—Rayce—standing in the doorway. "So...you are as powerful as they say," he murmured to Rayce. He'd heard the rumors, but...he didn't tend to believe rumors, not until he'd checked things out first-hand.

The tales about Luke and Leo? All true. Every blood-stained detail.

The rumors about Rayce being the most powerful werewolf to ever live? Still debatable, but the fact that he'd just snuck up on Cass...*I'll be watching you, wolf.*

"The angel is taken care of," Luke said again. "You don't need to waste your valuable talents on her now." His eyes gleamed. "Rayce has her in his sights."

"Damn right I do," the werewolf growled.

Cass rolled back his shoulders. "Why do I feel like this is an ambush?" Because it sure seemed that way. Luke was right in front of him. Rayce was at his back. "Did you invite me here so you could try to rip out my heart?" He waited a beat, then added, "Again?"

Luke laughed—not a good sign. "Don't tempt me."

Cass eased out a slow breath. "If you think you're bad enough…"

Luke's eyes began to glow. "We both know I am."

For just a moment, Cass could have sworn he saw the shadow of wings behind Luke's back. But when he blinked, the wings were gone. Luke had gotten himself back in control.

"I need you to find someone for me. Someone very, very important."

More important than a fallen angel? Curiosity had always been his weak spot and Luke *was* making him curious. But… "Before we say anything else, I want the wolf to move from behind me. I don't like having an enemy lurking at my back. Makes me…twitchy. And when I get twitchy, people get hurt." Cass thought that was a fair warning.

Luke inclined his head. Immediately, Rayce moved to the Lord of the Dark's side.

"I need to know you won't be in my way," Rayce fired at him. "I don't want to be tripping over the Reaper while I'm on my hunt."

The Reaper. Some titles just stuck. Cass raised his eyebrows. "Can't handle a little friendly competition?"

"Enough." Power hung in that one word from Luke—so much power that heat lanced over Cass's skin, but he didn't so much as flinch. He'd learned at a very young age never to show his pain.

He'd been six when he first learned that brutal lesson.

"You won't find the angel," Luke continued flatly. "She's not your mission, Reaper."

Ah, now Luke was calling him by the title, too. Definitely meant it was business time.

Luke's gaze seemed to bore into him. "I will pay you very, very well if you can bring the one I seek back to me."

Cass cocked his head to the right. "How well are we talking? Because your brother is offering me some very powerful magic in exchange for the angel—"

Luke laughed. The sound held no humor. "My brother is planning to betray you as soon as you deliver the angel back to him. He's learned the deadly mistake that can be made when you barter with magic, and he's not going to make that error again. He's promised you plenty, but

Leo will deliver nothing to you. He'll lock you away in a cage—remember what that was like? I bet you do—and then he'll only pull you out when he needs you again."

"Like I'm supposed to believe you?" Cass drawled. "You lie as easily as you breathe."

He saw Rayce's claws flash out.

"Careful there, wolf," Cass warned him. "You don't want to get on my bad side."

"And you don't want to get on mine," Luke replied before Rayce could speak. "I'm offering you a deal—a real one. And I've always kept my deals with you in the past."

Actually, that part was true. Luke might be a dangerous bastard, but he'd never broken a deal he'd made with Cass.

"I need you to hunt for me," Luke told him. "And unlike my brother, I *will* pay you in magic. Tell me what you want, and it's yours."

Temptation was there. Dark and twisting because it had been so very long for him. Too long. He looked down at his gloved hands. *Always have to be so careful. Always have to be alone. Always…*

"Get the wolf out of here, and we'll talk." Because okay—maybe Cass would make a deal with Luke. Maybe he would piss off Leo. Like he cared about the Lord of the Light. It had been a dull week—a dull decade—and he could use some excitement.

Cass could use a change.

"Before I leave, say you're not going after the angel. Say that first," Rayce ordered him.

Like he took orders from a werewolf? "Can't stand the competition, huh?"

"You will *not* touch her." Rayce took an aggressive step forward, but Luke's hand flew up, and his arm blocked Rayce before he could lunge for Cass.

Cass raised his chin. *My touch.* That was what so many feared and with good reason. "If Luke here can give me what I want, then I'll find his prey first."

First.

After he'd collected this bounty, then he'd turn his attention to Leo's job. "So you have a bit of a head start on me," Cass allowed. "Better use it."

Rayce growled again—and truly looked as if he'd like to use his claws to skin Cass. *Been there, done that before.*

"Go, Rayce," Luke said. "We have terms to make."

Still glaring, the werewolf left.

And then Cass was alone with the Lord of the Dark. They stared at each other. And Cass murmured, "I hear you've found love."

That muscle jerked in Luke's jaw again. "If you ever so much as come near my Mina, I will obliterate you."

Oh, wait—had the guy thought he was *threatening* him? No, Cass hadn't meant that part as a threat. Hell. "Even someone like you…" Someone who had a soul that had to be stained with blood. "You found a mate."

"Mina is special."

Mina must be insane, but whatever. Maybe Luke found insanity appealing. "I want that."

Luke grabbed him. His hand curled around Cass's throat and he heaved Cass up into the air—

"Not…her…" Cass choked out. "I want…*my*…*own*…*mate*…"

Luke threw him against the wall. Sheetrock spit into the air as Cass's body left a sizeable dent in the surface.

"Why didn't you say that?" Luke shook his head. "You should be more careful with me."

Noted. Cass brushed the dust off his shoulders. And his gaze dropped to his gloves once more. Gloves that had come to him—courtesy of Luke—very long ago. Cass had been hoping Leo would be able to give him an upgrade when he delivered the angel, but perhaps Luke could give him something far more valuable…"I want a woman who can stand my touch."

Now it was Luke's turn to laugh. "Why don't you just ask for a fucking unicorn? Because that would be easier—"

"I want a woman who can stand my touch. No gloves between us. No magic stopping my power. I want a woman I can touch..." His hands fisted. "And not kill."

Reaper.

Because that wasn't what he was—it was *who* he was. He was Death. He touched and he killed and no one could get close to him.

No one got close and survived, anyway.

Cass exhaled slowly. "If you can't do this for me, if you can't find a way, then I won't find the person you seek."

Silence.

"You got your Mina," Cass snarled when the silence stretched too long. "I've been on this earth for *centuries*. It's my turn. I am due. I want to touch—I want more than death."

Luke rubbed his chin. "Let me make sure I understand the terms of this deal...you want me to make sure there is a woman in this world who can survive your touch—and in turn, you'll bring me the person I seek? You'll turn her over to me, no questions asked and just walk away?"

"Yes."

Luke's hand flew out. "Deal."

Cass blinked. That had been...too easy.

Luke's hand just hung between them—waiting. Luke quirked a brow at him. "We must shake to agree. Just got to know you accept my terms and we can get this plan in motion."

Cass's gloved hand met Luke's. He shook. Another deal with the devil. "We didn't shake last time." He'd always wondered…would his touch kill Luke? If it didn't, he was sure that Luke would kill him, so Cass had never pushed that particular point of curiosity.

"Last time, I could have changed my mind on the deal." Luke smiled, a quick flash that showed no real humor. "But, lucky for you, I didn't." He freed Cass's hand and stepped back.

The deal was done. Cass exhaled slowly. He was eager to get hunting. The sooner he hunted, the sooner he had his mate. "Dead or alive?" Cass asked.

That was usually his first question when he took a job. With his particular skill set, dead was always the easier option.

"Alive."

So easy *wasn't* the word of the day.

"Who's the guy?" Cass wanted to know. "And sorry to be a dick, but why can't *you* find him? I mean, I thought you just snapped your fingers most days and all of the dark creatures had to do your bidding."

Doesn't work that way for me, though. Another deal…very long ago. Luke didn't control him.

"The prey you'll be seeking isn't dark. At least, not completely."

Interesting.

"And I never said you were hunting a man. You're after a woman. A very, very important woman."

"Does your Mina know this?" Cass murmured. Luke wanted him to find a woman—*a very, very important woman*—and bring her back alive? That was just—

Luke's eyes narrowed. "There is no sexual relationship between me and this prey."

Jeez. The guy actually sounded offended. "Whatever floats your boat, man."

The temperature in the room notched up again.

"Easy," Cass murmured.

"There isn't anything easy about me," Luke fired back. But he sucked in a sharp breath and seemed to regain his control. "Your prey is light and she is dark. A blend of both paranormal worlds."

Now that wasn't a combo Cass saw every day. "Give me a name. And if you have something of the woman's, that'd be helpful."

"Her name is Amber."

He waited. Nothing else came. The guy wanted to give him a challenge, huh? "And you have *nothing* of hers that I can use?"

Luke turned away. He paced toward his desk and opened a drawer there. For a moment, he just stared inside.

Cass tapped his foot.

Luke reached into the drawer and pulled out a small object. Then he headed back toward Cass, his fingers fisted around his prize.

Cass lifted up his gloved hand and held his palm out toward Luke.

Luke dropped a small, golden chain into Cass's hand. Even through the glove he wore, Cass could feel the heat of power. That chain—a bracelet—held powerful magic. His heartbeat stuttered a bit, a damn odd reaction for him, and he focused his gaze on the token he'd just been given.

He didn't have an enhanced sense of smell like shifters. He didn't track his prey that way. Instead, he relied on magic—on the imprints that people had left on objects they'd once possessed. Those objects acted as homing devices for him, pulling him straight to his prey.

Cass lifted his left hand, and with his teeth, he pulled off the glove. Then he shoved the glove into his pocket. His left hand—no longer shielded by anything—then reached for that bracelet. As soon as his fingers touched it, Cass let out a low hiss.

Pure power hit him.

But…

More than that. *She* hit him. For just an instant, her image flashed in his mind. Thick, long blonde hair. Eyes so gold and pure—seeing straight through him. She was tall and slim, her face unforgettable. She stared at him. He *felt* her.

Warm. Feminine.

And he wanted.

He'd *never* wanted a woman just because he'd touched an object that had once belonged to her. He'd never had a vision so strong. Never had his whole body react, but he *was* reacting. He'd gone into overdrive. Every single muscle in his body had clamped down. Desire beat in his blood, and Cass's heart galloped in his chest.

"Problem?" Luke demanded, watching him closely.

This time, Cass's hand was the one to fist around his prize. "I've got her." The woman with the golden eyes was in his mind now.

"Then bring her to me."

"And you'll give me what I want?" Cass asked the question automatically but…

The blonde woman's image flashed through his eyes once more. *Amber.*

"Absolutely." Luke smiled.

Cass grunted.

If you couldn't trust the devil, who could you trust?

CHAPTER ONE

The monsters were out in full force.

Amber Fortune—she'd recently picked the last name just because she liked the sound of it—took a moment to gaze around the packed bar. She counted five—no, *six*—vampires perched close to their would-be prey. The vamps were sporting fangs and even a bit of blood on their chins. They must have thought the blood was a sexy touch.

A werewolf was to her right, and his fur pushed out of his shirt. He wasn't sitting. Instead, the werewolf stood at his full height and every few moments, he let out a little howl.

Interesting.

There were some witches out there, oh-so-sexy witches with tight little skirts, high heels, and brooms at the ready. Their light laughter drifted in the air and invited others to join in with them.

"Another drink."

Amber's gaze swung to the mummy who'd appeared in front of her. His bandages were looking a little worn as he gave her a wide smile.

"Beer," he said, and his dark gaze slid over her. "Why aren't you dressed up? I mean…it's a Halloween party, right? Everyone is supposed to be dressed up?"

It was actually a pre-Halloween party since October 31st wouldn't be hitting for a few more days. But in New Orleans, the parties always started early.

She pushed a beer toward him. "I am wearing a costume." She glanced to the left, then to the right, and Amber leaned a bit over the bar, lowering her voice conspiratorially as she whispered, "The human skin? That's my costume. Underneath it, I'm the most terrifying monster you can imagine."

The mummy—probably a college guy from the looks of him—blinked a bit, as if he were trying to decide if she was joking.

She wasn't, but Amber gave him a wide smile.

Then he laughed. "Good one!" He saluted her with his beer bottle before he turned around and headed for the witches.

Good one. He had no idea.

Her short nails drummed on the bar top. Ten to one odds said the next person who walked into the bar would be wearing a vamp costume. Vamps were big this year. Ten to one—

The man who stalked through the doorway wasn't wearing a costume.

He had on jeans, a dark t-shirt and a dark hoodie. The hoodie was pulled up over his head, but she could see the hard angles of his face. The square jaw, the long, strong blade of his nose.

He was built with powerful shoulders and a tall, muscled frame. As she stared at him, Amber felt little alarm bells start to go off in her body.

Something is wrong. Something is—

He looked up at her, and Amber was immediately pinned by the bluest eyes she'd ever seen. Those eyes seemed to see right through her.

Breathe. Breathe. Be normal. But it was hard to be normal when fear was snaking through her insides. The stranger began walking toward her, and the crowd seemed to magically move right out of his path. He didn't touch anyone, not so much as a little brush of his shoulder against another person. He moved with a dark grace, and she should look away from him.

She didn't.

She also thought she should probably run.

She didn't.

She straightened her shoulders, lifted her chin, and let the music fade into the background as she faced the man who was coming right to her.

When he was about three feet from the bar, all of the vamps—and even the werewolf—suddenly got up and walked away. Coincidence? She didn't think so.

Who is he?

Her hand inched beneath the bar, searching for the weapon she liked to keep at the ready.

And then he was there, standing right in front of her. That too bright blue gaze of his swept over her face, seeming to absorb every detail of her expression. Then slowly, that gaze drifted down her body…or at least, it drifted over as much of her body as was visible before the bar hid her from his view.

"What do you want?" Amber wasn't just talking about drinks. This guy wasn't like the others in the bar. Goosebumps had risen on her arms. That tended to happen—when she was in the presence of another paranormal. It was part of her body's alarm system. She got cold when danger was near.

This guy—he was definitely dangerous.

The hood still covered his head, but she could see a hint of his dark hair. His skin was golden, his lips firm but oddly sensual, and up close, the guy seemed even bigger than he'd first appeared.

His hands lifted. He wore gloves—gloves that were black but didn't look to be made of leather. She wasn't sure *what* that material was.

His right hand flattened on the bar, but his left hand was fisted.

"I have something of yours."

Oh, wow. His voice. *His voice!* She'd never heard a voice so deep and dark. Even Vin Diesel couldn't compete with this guy. It wasn't just a voice that was heard. She swore she could *feel* that deep rumble in her body.

She was so distracted by his voice that it actually took a moment for his words to register, and when they did, Amber gave a sharp shake of her head. "I don't think so. You don't have anything that belongs to me—"

His fisted hand opened. She saw the gleam of gold. A bracelet. *Her* bracelet. A bracelet that she had not seen in a very, very long time. Because the last time she'd had that bracelet, it had been torn from her wrist. And the guy who'd ripped it off…

Oh, no.

"I can feel you in it," the stranger told her.

"That's weird," she said. "That is a seriously weird thing to say."

He blinked at her. For a moment, he looked a bit confused, but then his face just went back to that dangerous mask.

She smiled at him. "That is *not* my bracelet, so I don't think you should be feeling me anywhere near it."

"It's yours."

It was, yes. But Amber didn't plan to admit that fact anytime soon. "We have a lost and found here in the bar," she continued brightly. "Want me to put it in there? Maybe the owner will show up soon and claim it." Her hand reached out to swipe the bracelet from him. She was fast—so fast that she knew she'd be able to swipe the gold away before he could so much as—

His hand closed around hers, trapping her.

He's faster. Oh, crap. He is faster than I am.

"It's yours." Again, that deep voice of his rolled through her. His hold tightened on her hand. "I can *feel* you."

"Yes, well, that's because you're crushing my hand." He wasn't. He wasn't hurting her at all. "And I can feel you plenty, too."

He lifted their hands, staring at them with a look of what could have been wonder on his face. She was having a pretty hard time gauging the guy's expressions.

"You're warm and soft," he muttered. "It's almost as if...the glove isn't even there."

Had a psychotic paranormal just walked into her bar? Talk about bad luck.

"The glove *is* there." She glanced pointedly at their hands. "Now let me go."

He didn't. "What are you?" He'd leaned toward her and dropped his voice.

I'm a monster wearing human skin. Only if she said those words to him, Amber knew this fellow wouldn't laugh. "What are *you*?" she threw back at him.

"My enemies call me the Reaper."

Oh, for the love of...*The Reaper!* He was the Reaper? She could barely breathe and her goosebumps were back, but about a million times worse than they'd been before. She was *touching* the Reaper. Amber knew she had to get away from him. Far, far away, as fast as she possibly could.

Behind him, she saw a witch start to approach the bar. Before the woman got within three feet of the Reaper, though, she stiffened. Fear drifted over her face—a fear that Amber knew the woman would never be able to explain—and the witch turned and immediately walked back to her friends.

Even humans could sense when death was close.

"It's your bracelet." He still held her hand but he'd started to...stroke her wrist. Her pulse was racing beneath his gloved touch. She wanted to jerk her hand free, but Amber suspected he was stronger than she was. If she tried to jerk away, he'd just hold her tight. And then they'd both know he held all the power.

She had to take that power away.

She had to *get away.*

"I've been sent to find you," he added.

Yes, she'd figured as much. So she stopped pretending. "If you're the Reaper that I've heard about..." Heard about, been warned about, been told to stay far, *far* away from if she wanted to remain in the land of the living. "If you're that guy, then you're nothing more than a bounty hunter."

His lips curved the faintest bit. "A very highly paid bounty hunter."

"Dead or alive?" Her voice had gone husky.

His blue eyes seemed to heat.

"Isn't that the way it works for you? You bring in your victims dead...or alive?"

He shrugged one powerful shoulder. "Sometimes *undead* or alive."

Sweet hell. Her night was not looking good.

"You're not going to fight me," he continued. Did he even realize he was stroking her wrist? "You're not going to attract attention. You're going to just walk into the night with me, and you won't look back."

Oh, that was cute. He *was* delusional. She'd been right when she pegged him as a psychotic paranormal. "Luke sent you." Just when she'd thought he'd forgotten all about her.

The Reaper inclined his head. "The honor of your presence has been requested by the Lord of the Dark."

She smiled at him, and, much as she'd done with the human who'd been in that exact same spot just a few moments before, Amber leaned forward as if she were about to share a big secret with him. "Tell the Lord of the Dark…to go screw himself."

The Reaper blinked.

And Amber brought up the weapon she'd just palmed into her left hand. She yanked up the make-shift taser and shoved it against him as hard as she could. The volts of electricity pumped into him and he gave a jerk. He let her go because he had no choice—the Reaper was falling back and slamming into the floor.

She'd tinkered with that taser a bit. Amber had always been good at tinkering with things. So she'd given the device a paranormal upgrade. The taser wouldn't kill him. Actually, she wasn't sure anything *could* kill the Reaper, but it would give her a few precious moments to escape.

The costumed humans—at least those within a ten-foot radius—had turned to stare at the fallen man in shock. Amber didn't waste time staring. She leapt over the bar in one very agile jump. She landed on her feet and prepared to race for freedom.

But his gloved hand curled around her foot. "Not…so fast…"

She smiled at him. "Want more?" Then she gave him another shock. He cursed her as his body shuddered. But even as he jerked and twitched, he yanked the taser from her hand. *His strength is going to be a problem.*

Amber broke free from him and raced for the doorway. She shoved the humans out of her path and tasted sweet, sweet freedom as she burst out of the bar.

***

"Dude…" A vampire stared down at him. A vampire with crooked fangs. "She totally tased your ass. Twice."

Cass narrowed his eyes on the vampire. Then he rose, slowly. When Amber had tased him for the second time, Cass had yanked the taser from her. Now, he crushed it in his gloved hands. Crushed it to dust. "Where…is…she?"

The vampire pointed toward the door.

Cass would find her. He'd follow her. He had her bracelet after all, so that meant tracking her wouldn't be any challenge at all to him and—

No, hell, no. Cass did a quick search.

Amber had taken the bracelet. She'd tased him with one hand and stolen the bracelet with the other. Talk about tricky.

And impressive.

Without the bracelet, he'd just have to do things the old fashioned way. No more magic beacon right to him. But, he *would* find her. He'd just have to work harder.

Because she was *not* getting away. He always brought back his bounties. Always.

She would be no different.

CHAPTER TWO

She'd tossed everything she owned into a small, black suitcase. Everything *including* the bracelet she'd retrieved from the bar. Amber rushed through the alley behind her building, clutching that suitcase as if her life depended on it. She had to get out of New Orleans. She loved the city, but it was time to move on. When the Reaper came calling, it was definitely time to head the hell out. Maybe hanging in New Orleans had been her mistake. She'd lingered too long in the Big Easy. She usually only stayed in a city for around three months, then she shipped out.

She'd been in New Orleans for six. She'd gotten too complacent. Too certain that Luke didn't give a flying fuck about where she was or what she was doing.

Oh, how very wrong she'd been.

Amber's footsteps were silent as she dodged a dumpster and slipped around the corner. Her car waited just on the next street, tucked away in the parking garage there and—

"Going somewhere?"

She bit back a startled scream because *he* was suddenly looming out of the dark. The Reaper. Looking big and pissed and dangerous. He still had his hood covering his head, and he was still making goosebumps rise on her arms.

Amber staggered to a halt before she barreled into him. Touching him again was *not* on her to-do list. Not if all those tales about him were true. "Stay away from me!" Maybe she should throw her suitcase at him and run.

"Why? Do you have another taser on you?"

Unfortunately, no. Dammit. And since she *didn't* have a weapon handy, she *did* throw her suitcase at him. It slammed into his chest and bounced before hitting the ground.

He blinked. Then he focused those too-bright-to-be-real blue eyes on her suitcase, before looking back up at her. "Why did you do that?"

"Because you're pissing me off!"

"And anger is your response?" He shook his head and made a tut-tut-tut sound. "You need to work on that anger management issue."

How fast could he run? She didn't have enhanced speed. These days, she barely seemed to have any paranormal bonuses. But if she turned around and ran, would he grab her instantly?

"Come on." He waved toward her with an impatient flick of his gloved hand. "We need to go. Luke is waiting, and the sooner I finish up this job, then the sooner I get what I want."

And the sooner she had a swift trip to hell. *No, thank you.* She retreated one small step, her shoe sliding over the broken cement beneath her. "I can pay you," Amber blurted, desperate.

His eyes narrowed. That stare raked over her.

"Whatever Luke is offering, I can double it." A total lie. She barely had any cash.

"I don't think you can give me what I need." His hands went to his hips. "But thanks for the offer. It was tempting."

Sonofa—

She turned and ran. As fast as she could and it just *wasn't* fast enough because the Reaper grabbed her with those gloved hands of his and yanked her back. Before she could even get the breath to scream—she'd always been a good screamer—he'd shoved her against the dirty, brick wall of that alley. He pinned her between the bricks and his body, and his hands pressed hers back, holding her captive easily. Too easily.

"I am not in the mood for a chase." Each word was gritted and his face had turned even harder. "If I have to do it, I will tie you up and gag you and you can travel that way for the entire trip back to Key West."

"That's kidnapping," she whispered.

He shrugged. "That's collecting a paranormal bounty."

Play this angle. Do this. "I'm…I'm not a paranormal."

And there it was—the briefest of hesitations. His grip on her eased a little bit. Not enough for her to escape, but just enough for her to know that the guy wasn't super comfortable with the idea of abducting a human.

Oh, sure. He'd take a paranormal…*Like we don't matter?* But when he thought he might be capturing a human, it became a whole new ball game.

"You…are." But he didn't sound convinced.

"I'm not. I'm not a shifter or a vampire." She opened her mouth wide, showing her normal teeth. "I'm not a witch or a siren or anything like that." Her heart raced in her chest. "Luke is trying to turn me into something I don't want to be. Please, *please* help me. Let me walk away. Tell him that you never found me."

He—he brought his face down even closer to her. And his mouth hovered right over her neck. What was he doing? Was he—

Smelling her?

"Honey."

Amber froze.

"You smell like honey…and champagne."

She licked her lips. "I, um, spilled a little champagne when I opened a bottle for a customer earlier."

He gave a low growl. Was that rough sound supposed to be some kind of question or something? Or—

He put his mouth on her neck.

"Don't! Don't kill me!"

But it was too late. He'd pressed his lips to the curve of her throat. He was...kissing her neck. Lightly licking the skin. And as crazy as it was...heat began to unfurl deep within her.

"You taste like honey...and champagne."

Her breath heaved out.

His head lifted. His eyes seemed a little brighter. "And my mouth won't kill you, sweets. It's my hands that do that. I could put my mouth over every single inch of you, and I guarantee, you'd only know pleasure. Not death."

Oh, *shit.* His words should *not* be turning her on, but she'd always been wired a little bit *wrong.* So his words—they made her hot.

Wrong, wrong, wrong.

But...since he was doing this whole sniffing and tasting routine, then maybe he believed her about being human. "I'm not a paranormal. You've never smelled anyone like me...you've never tasted anyone like me." Because there was no other like she was. "Luke is tricking you. Using you. It's what he does. You can't trust the devil, everyone knows that."

The Reaper had pulled back so that he could stare down at her. Jeez but the guy was *big*. Muscled. Those shoulders of his were so wide.

"Let me go." She injected a plea in her voice. "Just tell Luke that you couldn't find me."

And he...

Shook his head.

Dammit.

"You're coming with me. I'll deliver you to him—*that* was my deal. I get what I want when Luke has you."

Hell. Her lips parted. If there was no other option, then she'd scream—

"But if you're telling the truth, if you *are* human, I won't let him hurt you."

She bit back her scream. *The Reaper definitely has a weak spot for humans.* So she'd play that card a little longer. Maybe if she acted as if she were cooperating, it would buy her a chance at freedom.

Maybe...

"We're leaving the city tonight. I have a plane waiting for us. We'll be back in Key West in time to see the sunrise."

No way. She had no intention of going back there.

Then his right hand moved in a fast blur and Amber felt something snap along her right wrist. She felt a hot brand, could have sworn her skin actually sizzled for a moment, and she became aware of the cold weight of metal against her wrist.

Handcuffs. One cuff was around her wrist. The other was around his. Her right wrist. His left.

"You are a serious sonofabitch," Amber muttered.

"The cuffs are paranormal proof," he said, inclining his head. "Just in case you're, you know, lying to me about *not* being a paranormal. Even shifters can't break out of them and you don't exactly strike me as having a shifter's strength. If you did, I think you would have punched me back at the bar and not used your little taser."

That *little* taser had knocked him on his ass.

He started walking back down the alley. Since they were now linked, she had to walk, too. He paused just a moment and bent to pick up her suitcase. Was that supposed to be kind of him? She was so angry that Amber was pretty sure steam was rising from her skin.

Oh, no, wait, that wasn't steam. It was smoke coming from that weird hand-cuff. "It…hurts." *Burns.*

"That's because it's locking you down. It's linking us. In just a few minutes, it will disappear, and after that, you won't be able to move more than five feet away from me."

What?

She grabbed his arm. "Where does it disappear to, exactly?"

Sighing, he looked back at her. "They're magic cuffs. They lock around us both, and they link us both. Right now, they're linking—that's why you feel as if you're burning. The cuffs are creating a special tie between us. You won't be able to escape me."

Not good. "That tie can't last forever. I mean, once you deliver me to Luke, how do you get rid of the link, then?"

He leaned toward her. His lips brushed against her ear as he said, "*Magic.*" He gave a low laugh. "Did you miss that part?"

Asshole. He was such an—

"Where is she?" The deep bellow seemed to shake the alley itself. It was a rough rumble of sound and one that was heartbreakingly familiar to her.

A man had appeared—seemingly falling right out of the sky to land a few feet in front of the Reaper. The man had midnight black hair and golden eyes. Power radiated from him.

Power. Danger.

Magic.

Maybe a touch of madness.

Amber immediately slid behind the Reaper.

"Where is my angel?" the man demanded.

Not a man, not really. She'd recognized the fellow on sight, even though it had been a *very* long time since she'd had the displeasure of his company. Amber was staring at none other than Leo, the so-called Lord of the Light.

Luke and Leo were the all-powerful twins who thought they ruled the world.

Leo was supposed to be on the side of the good.

Luke was on the side of the bad. The very, very bad.

In her book, they were both trouble.

"You came rushing to the Big Easy. I know you were tracking her." Leo's voice boomed out again. *"Where is the angel?"*

"Yeah, about that..." the Reaper drawled. "I'm not working that case any longer. Better find yourself a new hunter."

Wait, hold up. The Reaper was supposed to track an *angel* for Leo? How had Leo lost an angel? She almost smiled. Oh, she bet that loss hurt him.

"Cass..." Leo's voice had grown cold. "You won't want to play with me."

So the Reaper had a regular name. *Cass.* Amber kind of liked it. Right then, she kind of liked him—because he stood between her and Leo. Leo hadn't focused on her, not yet, and she knew it was because the spell she'd put in place to protect herself was still working. A spell specifically designed to shield her from Luke...and Leo.

How much distance remained between them? Ten feet? Had to be…but if he came closer…

The spell was designed so that neither Luke nor Leo would ever be able to find me. The wizard promised me they couldn't get within ten feet of me.

Like, literally. Luke and Leo could *not* even see her…unless they happened to be within ten feet of her. But if they passed that ten-foot mark, if they came close enough, if they actually stumbled upon her…*all bets are off.*

She crouched down, hunching her body so that she could totally disappear behind the Reaper—um, Cass.

But then she heard the soft rustle of Leo's footsteps coming closer. "You've got a bounty behind you."

"She's of no concern to you."

Amber tugged on the stupid, magical handcuff. Still visible. Still slightly burning her. When she tugged, she automatically jerked Cass's hand back toward her.

"Are you hiding my angel?" Now Leo's voice roughened even more. Odd, the normally polished Leo didn't usually sound as if he were biting nails. But it *had* been a few decades since she'd seen him. Maybe he'd changed.

Doubtful.

"She's not yours. This bounty has *nothing* to do with you so step out of my way. I told you...you need to find someone else for your angel job. I'm not working for you."

The rustle came again. Leo—moving closer. Eliminating that all-important ten-foot rule that had kept her protected for so long.

She heard Leo's sharp inhale. Now that he was closer and past that magical barrier, he'd be able catch her scent. And when Cass moved, Leo would see her.

I'm done.

"Please," she whispered to Cass, so desperate that she would have tried anything. "Don't let him take me."

Cass swung back toward her in surprise. "Why would Leo want you?"

"Amber."

The instant Cass had moved, she'd fallen into Leo's line of sight. He raced forward, his arms outstretched.

He was coming for her. He was—

A couple of things happened very, very fast.

First...Cass yanked off the glove that covered his right hand. The hand that was *not* cuffed to hers.

Second...the glove hit the ground.

Third...Cass lifted his uncovered hand toward Leo.

"Ready to die?" Cass asked the Lord of the Light.

Leo froze, jerking to a halt that appeared to be just *inches* from Cass's outstretched hand.

"Because I can take down just about any paranormal being that walks on this earth," Cass told him flatly. "And I'm thinking…if Luke is afraid for me to touch him, then you have to fear me, too."

Was that true? Did Luke fear his touch?

Leo started sweating. His gaze darted from Cass's uncovered hand to her face. "Amber," Leo whispered. "I've searched for you."

"And I've hidden from you." From him and from Luke—for very good reason. *I never wanted to be found. I don't want to be a part of your war…or your world.*

Leo shook his head. "You don't need to be afraid."

She absolutely did.

Leo's gaze flew back to Cass. "Luke hired you to find her."

"I don't like discussing my clients," Cass murmured. "All you need to know is that I'm no longer hunting your angel. Find someone else—and actually, you'd better hurry with that hunt. Because the last time I checked, a certain werewolf was intent on finding her."

Leo shook his head. "Lila can wait. I need Amber."

Amber was shaking—with fear and anger and too many other emotions she didn't want to think about. "We have to get out of here," Amber said to Cass. "You can't trust him. He'll turn on you."

"Amber!" Leo called out.

She stared straight into Leo's eyes. "You turned on me. Just when I needed you the most."

"Because you chose *him!* What was I supposed to do? You gave him—"

"Get me out of here," Amber cut through Leo's words before he could say too much. "Reaper, I will agree to *any* deal you want—just get us away."

Cass gave one hard nod and kept his stare on Leo. "You're in my way."

The air in that alley seemed to heat. Leo's shoulders stiffened. "You don't want me as an enemy, Reaper."

"No? Well, since I'm not exactly in the market for friends and I don't generally give a damn about enemies, how about you just get the hell out of my way...before I *make* you move."

Leo's chin jutted into the air. "Try it. She's worth it. I will fight—"

White light shot out of Cass's hand and hit Leo dead center in the chest. Leo flew up into the air—then he flew back and went crashing toward another dumpster. Amber didn't even get to see him land. Cass had grabbed his discarded glove, he'd snagged her suitcase again, and he'd started running down that alley. She ran with him, more than happy to get away from Leo and put that all important ten-foot rule into place once more.

Now you see me…now you don't.

Her breath heaved from her as they burst out of the alley and she found a dark SUV waiting for her.

Cass threw her suitcase into the backseat and then he yanked open the driver's side door. "Get in and get buckled."

Automatically, she glanced down at the handcuffs, wondering how she was supposed to manage that maneuver.

But the handcuff had vanished.

"Consider it a five-foot tether. You can't get away from me now."

Five feet…I have to stay near the Reaper.

Ten feet…Luke and Leo can't find me.

"Time's up," Cass growled. "Get that sweet ass in the vehicle before I have to kill the Lord of the Light for you."

I don't want him dead.

She shimmied across to the passenger seat. Cass jumped in behind her. He revved that engine and they shot away with a squeal of tires. The headlights cut across the dark road and she saw—

Wings. Big, powerful wings stretching from Leo's back. The Lord of the Light was in the middle of the road and he looked *pissed.* So pissed that he'd slipped up and let his wings out. *In public.*

"Amber!" Leo roared her name.

"What in the hell is it with you?" Cass demanded. "The two most powerful beings in the world are *both* after you?"

It would appear that was the case.

The SUV lurched forward, heading right for Leo. Horrified, she glanced over at Cass.

"Let's play a little chicken," he said and there was a smile on his face. Wild and reckless.

No wonder he'd wanted her to buckle her seatbelt. He was insane. *Psychopath paranormal.* She'd pegged him right from the first moment.

The SUV barreled straight for Leo. The headlights showed his shock and then—

They hit him. Leo went spinning into the air once more, and she was pretty sure he'd left a major dent in the front of the SUV, but Cass didn't slow down. Amber looked back, expecting to see the Lord of the Light rising from the pavement. But, no...

Leo had vanished.

CHAPTER THREE

"I…thought we were flying out of New Orleans." Amber stood in the middle of the hotel room, her hands crossed over her chest. "But…here we are, bunking down for the night in Biloxi."

Cass swept his gaze over her and then he stalked closer to Amber, eliminating that five feet of distance. She stiffened as Cass approached, and he caught the tell-tale movement. Amber was afraid of him. Good. She should be afraid.

Liars pissed him off.

He stopped right in front of her. "Change of plans. I figured your buddy Leo would be looking for us at the airports in the immediate area, so driving away from New Orleans seemed like the best idea."

"Leo is *not* my buddy."

"Then what the hell is he?"

Her lips—sexy, full, plump lips that made him think of all sorts of dark ideas—pressed together.

Cass laughed. "Really? You think you don't get to answer? Come on…I'm just dying to hear why two of the most powerful paranormal beings on earth are about to seriously lose their shit when it comes to you."

Her long lashes shielded her gaze.

She was obviously trying to think of a plausible lie. *Good luck with that, sweets.* While she thought of her lie, he studied her. Her hair was heavy and golden—not a light blonde but so much richer and darker. Her skin was even golden, as if it had been kissed by the sun.

Kissed? What in the hell is wrong with me? I don't think that fucking way.

He growled.

Her gaze immediately jerked back to his.

Her face wasn't perfect. He kept telling himself that. Her cheeks were a little too high. Her chin was a little too sharp. Her nose was a little—

Hell. She's sexy. Her face comes together—it's better than perfect. I see her and I don't want to look away. I see her…and I want.

His gloves were both back in place so he lifted his right hand and cupped her cheek. He could feel the silk of her skin even through the magical fabric. "Want to tell me…" His voice had gone darker. "Why the Lord of the Dark and his brother are both after a human?"

"I…they think I have something that belongs to them."

Truth? Or lie? Cass was betting lie.

She backed up a step. "I don't, but they won't believe me. They think I have what they need, and they're determined to get it back, no matter the cost."

He advanced on her.

Again, she retreated.

Did she realize that if she took even one more step back, that she'd be bumping into the king bed that dominated that room? He'd gotten them a room at one of the bigger hotels in Biloxi, one with a floor-to-ceiling window that gave them a killer view of the beach. Their hotel was connected to the nearby casino, and the room was usually reserved for high-rollers.

"What do you have?" Cass asked her.

Again, she retreated. Only this time, Amber bumped into the bed. She glanced down, then looked back up, her face utterly horrified.

Right. That was generally the look women got when they found themselves in close proximity to a bed and to the Reaper. He smiled at her. "What do you have, sweets?" Cass asked again, truly curious to hear her answer. "It must be something very powerful."

She licked her lips. His cock jerked. *Down. Fucking down.*

"Why?" Amber asked. "Do you want it for yourself?"

His gaze swept over her body. High, round breasts. Long, long legs…And her scent was teasing him. Driving him wild. Cass knew something he wanted all right, but he couldn't have it.

She cleared her throat. "Look, Reaper—I mean, um, Cass—thanks for getting me away from Leo. I super appreciate that—"

He grunted. He wanted more than her appreciation.

"But, and trust me on this, you don't want to get in the middle of this war. And coming between Luke and Leo? That will rip you apart. Or *they* will." She shook her head. "I'm speaking from experience, okay? You don't want to mess with them. Be smart. Just walk away. Leave me here and vanish."

"Luke couldn't find you."

Her face immediately became shuttered.

"I asked him why he couldn't find you on his own, why he needed me and he said it was because you weren't dark."

Her hands twisted in front of her.

"You weren't dark, not completely, and I'm guessing Leo can't locate you for the same reason, huh? You're not completely good? You're hidden from them both, and Leo only discovered you today because he'd been tailing me."

She wasn't just twisting her hands any longer. Now, Amber was rubbing her right wrist. Probably trying to rub off that now invisible handcuff. *Won't happen, sweets. You can't get free of that.*

Red stained her cheeks. "No, they can't find me, not normally. But obviously, Leo can find *you*. And now because of your handcuff mumbo-jumbo, he's going to be able to find me, too. Unless you go away. Leave. But do your magic first and unhook us, okay? Then you'll be safe, and I'll disappear."

He stepped toward her. There was nowhere for her to retreat now. Not unless she wanted to fall onto the bed.

Her head tipped back as she stared up at him.

Once more, his gloved hand lifted to stroke her cheek. Why did he like touching her so much?

Because touching has always been forbidden.

But…there was more, with her. Normally, he couldn't feel when he used the gloves. He had no sensation in his fingers. But when he touched her, it was as if the gloves didn't exist. He could feel her warmth. Could feel the softness of her skin.

Heaven.

His head lowered over hers. Her lips were so close to his. When he'd been trying to decide if she was human or if she was a paranormal, he'd bent close to inhale her scent. Even though his nose wasn't nearly as strong as a shifter's, sometimes, he could pick up the scent of another paranormal.

But then he'd gone a step beyond and he'd put his mouth on her. Not because of some BS about being able to *taste* whether she was paranormal or human. Just because he'd wanted to put his mouth on her. Staring at her lips right then—that plump lower lip, that sexy-bow-shaped top lip—he wanted to kiss her.

His kiss wouldn't kill. Despite the stories out there, only his hands held the power to kill. She'd be perfectly safe if he kissed her. Or if he put his mouth on other parts of her luscious body. Oh, the things he could do to her with his mouth.

"Cass?"

Her voice had gone husky. He liked it when she said his name.

"Th-that is what Leo called you, right? Because I'd rather say Cass than Reaper—"

"My name is Cassius. Cassius Garvan."

Her lips curled. "Cass to your friends?"

"And Reaper to my enemies."

She stared straight into his eyes. "And to your lovers? What do they get to call you?"

Did she realize how dangerous it was to taunt him? He didn't answer her.

Amber swallowed, and he saw the delicate movement of her throat. "Cass, look, despite the whole death-touch thing that you have going on, I don't think you're a bad person."

She thought wrong.

"I mean, you helped me get away from Leo. That was solid, and I appreciate what you did."

Were they back to that? "I don't want your appreciation."

A furrow appeared between her eyes. "Then what do you want? I offered to pay you before—"

"I want to taste you." The words came out, unplanned, but truer than anything he'd said to her before. "I want your mouth beneath mine."

Her gaze slid to his lips. Had her pupils widened? He thought they had, and her scent seemed to have deepened. But she didn't look afraid.

She looked…curious. "Is your kiss safe?" Amber asked him.

His heart jerked hard in his chest.

"I don't know what that crazy light was that shot from your hand. I've never…met a Reaper before."

His lips hitched into a half-smile. "Generally, that's because most people don't live to tell that particular meet-and-greet story."

Her eyes widened.

Fear.

He didn't like her fear. "There aren't many of my kind left." He gave a bitter laugh. "Actually, as far as I know, I *am* the last of my kind."

Her lips parted. "Oh. I-I'm sorry. I—I understand." And her hand reached up, as if she were going to touch *him*. Willingly. It looked as if she'd give him a pat on the shoulder, but then her hand stilled, mid-air.

Every muscle in his body turned to stone. "You can touch me."

She bit that delectable lower lip. "You sure about that?"

"It's only my hands that have the power to kill. You can kiss me and be safe."

"*I'm* not so sure about that," Amber muttered.

"You can touch me," he continued darkly, "and be safe." Though hardly anyone ever had touched him. Why touch Death? People feared Death too much to ever want to get close. She feared him, too. She wouldn't trust his word. She wouldn't—

Her fingers curled around his shoulder. He felt that light touch sink beneath his skin and brush against what remained of his soul.

"Cass? I'm...I'm sorry that you're alone. I know what that's like."

She had no clue.

But he couldn't look away from her mouth. She was the first woman—the first to ever touch him so easily. He hadn't needed to bribe her, hadn't needed to promise her power or protection. She'd touched him to comfort him.

And she made him ache.

"Cass?"

"I want to kiss you."

He heard the little hitch in her breathing. "No."

His body tightened at the rejection.

"No," she said again and her hand fell away from him. He missed that touch immediately. "No, you don't want to kiss me. You don't want me at all. I'm just some bounty to you, and you're playing some dangerous game with me. But you don't want this game, okay? You need to break the invisible cuffs or whatever the hell they are. Use the magic you talked about and set us both free."

He couldn't look away from her mouth. "I may have misled you."

"Yes, I know. I just said you don't really want to kiss me—"

"I can't break the spell that locked the cuffs in place. They will link us for forty-eight hours, no matter what I do." His delivery guarantee. He'd used the cuffs hundreds of times. Normally, forty-eight hours was all he needed for transport. He took in his prey, he kept the prey close, and when the forty-eight hours ended, he walked away clean.

His prey didn't fare as easily. They often didn't walk away at all.

"Forty-eight hours?" she repeated, voice hushed. "No, no, that's too long! Leo will find you again!"

Cass laughed. "I don't think so. Not if I don't want to be found." His gaze slowly rose to catch hers.

Hope lit her stare. "You…you can actually hide us from him?"

"I'm not working for Leo. He won't get you." That was a promise.

She threw her body against his. "Thank you!"

Cass was so caught off-guard by her move that he froze. Her arms were wrapped around him. She was *hugging* him, and her breasts pressed to his chest. Her whole body pressed to him, and she felt warm and she smelled good and his dick was hard with desire and he wanted to hold her tight—

She looked up at him. "Sorry. But, um, you said you were safe to touch and—"

His control shattered. He'd *never* had someone embrace him that way. Yes, she'd just been hugging him, he got that. She'd been caught up in her relief. He got *that*.

Cass just didn't care.

His arms closed around her, and they tumbled back onto the bed. His gloved hands sank into the thick mass of her hair and his lips crashed down on hers. He knew he should be more careful, he should use more restraint, but…

His control had shattered. All of the needs he'd held in check for so long burst free and he had to kiss her. His mouth locked to hers. Her lips parted beneath his mouth, and her tongue swept out to meet his.

She wasn't afraid. Wasn't hesitant. Amber kissed him with a raw need that ignited the dark desires he'd held back for too long. Finally, someone who wasn't afraid. Finally, someone who wanted him.

He kissed her deeper, harder. Her clothes were between them. His were in the way. He wanted the clothes gone. He wanted them to be flesh to flesh.

He. Wanted. Her.

She gave a little moan and arched up against him. Her hands raked down his back. Her nails bit into his skin. Her lips parted even more as she kissed him and he—

Stopped.

Cass slowly lifted his head. His gaze met hers. His breath heaved in his chest. "What kind of game are you playing?"

She licked the lips he'd just tasted. "What?"

"You think if you act like you want me, I'll let you go?"

Her pink cheeks darkened even more. "You're the one who said you wanted to kiss me!"

His legs were between her spread thighs. His hands pushed down on either side of her head. He trapped her beneath him. "I'm the one who wants to fuck you."

Her pupils definitely expanded. The gold was almost swallowed by the darkness.

"And you expect me to believe," his voice rasped at her, "that you're the woman who actually wants Death?" He wasn't stupid, and this wasn't the first time prey had tried to trick him for freedom.

"I'm the woman who's staring up at an idiot," she snapped.

Cass frowned.

"Get the hell off me!" Then she didn't wait for him to comply. She shoved against him, hard. Not hard enough to move him. Maybe she *was* human, after all. Because she sure didn't seem to have any paranormal strength.

But Cass moved off her. It was either move or give in to the dark lust snaking through his body. He stood by the side of the bed.

She glared up at him.

"Kissing me won't give you freedom," he warned her.

Her jaw dropped. Then it snapped closed. Then *she* was on her feet and jabbing her index finger into his chest. "You kissed me, Reaper. Get that fact straight. You. Kissed. Me. You pushed me onto the bed. You put your mouth on mine. And you were giving me a pretty good kiss—"

Wait. Had she just said only "pretty good"? He actually felt his cheeks burn.

"Then you just blew things to hell." In apparent disgust, she threw her hands up into the air. "Do you just have no tact or no sense? Because when a woman kisses you and you act as if she's doing it as some kind of payment or bribe…well, that tends to make a woman feel like crap."

"I…" He was in way over his head.

"I kissed you because—and this will sound crazy, I know, given our circumstances—I wanted to see what it would be like."

So did I.

Only, apparently, she'd just thought it was just "pretty good." Hell. A woman like her probably kissed plenty of men. She had dozens of lovers. Men who would jump if she crooked her finger. Men who would—

"Why are you growling? And are your hands fisting?"

He was growling because he was angry. No, *jealous* of the unknown men who'd been lucky enough to be near her. His hands were fisting because he was imagining driving his bare hand into the faces of those jerks. Death punch.

"Cass?"

He tried to get his shit together, but his mind was in chaos. The lust still rode him just as hard and his dick was about to shove right out of his jeans. He was *not* cooling down. "Come with me." Then he turned on his heel and headed for the bathroom.

"What? Are you crazy? I—ah!"

He looked back and saw her stumbling forward, her right wrist out as she was pulled after him. "Five feet is the limit. I think you can stand outside of the door."

He marched into the bathroom. She had to follow—at least to the door.

"Wait!" Amber cried out, her voice sharp. "You're going to use the bathroom? In the middle of our fight? You are so weird! This isn't normal. Not at all!"

Nothing about him was normal. He yanked on the cold water faucet, sending water plummeting down into the narrow shower stall.

Then he started stripping.

"What are you *doing?*"

He thought it was pretty obvious. "Cooling down." Because the lust he felt for her was too strong. He had to get his control back, ASAP.

He left his clothes in a pile and stepped under the water.

CHAPTER FOUR

"Man, I am telling you…it was the craziest shit I ever saw!" The vampire paused as his buddy propped his shoulder against the nearby alley wall. "The bartender—you know, that pretty number with the blonde hair—she pulled out her taser and knocked that guy on his ass! She didn't just hit the bruiser once. She did it twice. Then the guy—he just got up. Like it was nothing. He *walked* out of the bar without even a second glance. It was like…freaking *Halloween* shit. He was all Michael Myers up in that place!"

"No way." His friend was disbelieving. "You are drunk off your ass and making up crap again. You *always* do this." He waved toward the vamp. "Go sober up. I'll see you Monday in Chemistry." Then he turned and walked away.

"It is not bullshit!" the vampire yelled after him. "That shit is real! It happened. The guy must have been freaking superhuman the way he just jumped back up. Like a horror movie villain or something—and did I mention he was wearing a hood the whole time? A hood and gloves and—"

"I don't think your story is bullshit," Leo announced, tired of hiding in the shadows and just listening to the drunk vampire's story.

The vampire gave a high-pitched yell and then he spun to face Leo. The vamp actually clutched his chest.

Not a real vamp, of course. The blood on the side of his mouth was fake. The fangs were fake. Leo was just looking at a scared frat boy. A human, so Leo would go easy on him. This human wasn't bad. Just drunk.

"Don't sneak up on people!" the drunk vamp said—only his words came out in a too fast tumble.

Leo lifted a brow. "I want to hear more about your story." He waved his hand toward the human. "Tell me everything you remember about the man in the hood."

The human blinked, once, twice, then he started speaking because he had to follow Leo's command. "He was about six foot two, maybe three. He wore a gray hoodie over his head, but I saw his eyes. They were bright blue. He had on gloves—black gloves. Looked like leather, but I don't know if they were."

"They weren't." They were made of something far more valuable. "Keep going."

"He went to see the bartender. Only had eyes for Amber."

"Because she's his prey." *But he won't keep her. He'll just deliver her to Luke.*

"She tased him and ran. I don't think she liked him."

She might not like him, but she'd sought the Reaper's protection when she could have gone with Leo. *She still hates me that much.* His chest ached, and Leo rubbed the area over his heart. Few would believe he had a heart.

He did. And Amber owned a very large piece of it.

"Do you know anything else useful?" Leo's head cocked. "Do you happen to know where Amber lived?"

"Near Jackson Square. In the apartment over the bookstore. I…saw her there one day, when I was out for a jog. A woman like her is hard to miss."

"Yes. She is." He stared at the human. "But you're going to forget her. You'll forget Amber. You'll forget the man in the hood. You will walk your ass home and sleep off the booze."

The vampire nodded. Then he turned away and began walking down the street. Leo waited until the human was out of sight, and then he took to the sky, shooting high up and rushing away. Leo didn't look back. He didn't look down…

His thoughts were focused completely on Amber. He had to find her. Had to get to her…before the Reaper delivered Amber back to his brother.

Amber had almost died because of Luke once before. He would *not* let Luke hurt her again.

***

A weakness.

Gregory Cethin watched from the rooftop as the Lord of the Light flew away. It had been pure chance that he'd been in New Orleans when Leo had come calling. When he'd seen the SUV barreling down the road, when he'd seen the mighty Leo go flying after impact…

Priceless. So he'd just had to hang around. Just had to see what wonders waited for him.

And now, Gregory had a most precious prize. Leo was gone now, vanishing into the sky, but the human was still close by. He jumped from the building and his knees barely buckled when he touched down on the street below. Whistling, he closed in on his prey.

"I like the cape," he called out to the human.

The guy spun toward him.

"Ah…the fangs are a nice touch, too," Gregory said. "Gives that realistic edge that vamps need." He tapped his own fangs. "I mean, how can you bite, without the fangs?"

The human frowned at him. "Do I know you?"

He stalked forward, closing the distance between them and clamping his hand over the human's shoulder. "You and I…we're going to be very close."

"I need to get home—I'm supposed to sleep—"

"You're going to tell me all about the woman named Amber. You're going to tell me why Leo was after her…and then you're going to tell me where I can find her."

But the human yanked out his fake fangs. "Look, buddy, I don't know anything—"

No, he probably didn't, if Leo's compulsion had wiggled into his brain. It was a good thing that Gregory knew how to work around that pesky compulsion. "Wrong answer." Gregory jerked the human forward and sank his teeth into the fellow's throat. Unlike the frat boy, he didn't have fake fangs. His razor sharp teeth sliced deep. The human tried to scream, but Gregory just clamped his hand over the guy's mouth. He drank deep, taking plenty of that sweet blood. And then, when he was sure his victim was too weak to fight, he pulled his teeth out of the guy's throat.

"Now let's try that again," Gregory murmured. His hand rose from the human's mouth as he gazed at the fool. He'd just made a blood bond between them. A bond that would shatter Leo's compulsion. "You *will* tell me what I want to know..."

Because he'd spent years searching for a tool that he could use against Leo and his asshole brother Luke. And if he'd finally found a weapon in his battle...

I will use her until there is nothing left. I will use her, and the twins will be destroyed.

Leo had applied his mind control magic on the human, but Gregory had just created a blood bond between them. He *would* get the truth from the human...and if the guy resisted too hard, then Gregory would just fucking kill him.

Why would he care if another human died?

If he had his way...Leo would die, too. Leo...Luke...everyone in his way.

Because Gregory had plans. Big, fucking plans...and it was time for him to take the power that had always been destined to be his.

CHAPTER FIVE

Staring was rude. She shouldn't stare. Amber knew that.

But...something else that was rude? Kidnapping a woman. Handcuffing her with magic.

Stripping in front of her.

So if Cass didn't want her staring at his awesome ass, then maybe he shouldn't have handcuffed her in the first place. Or stripped.

So Amber just propped her shoulders against the door frame and stared through the glass shower door at Cass. There was no steam drifting in the air—nothing to block her vision. From what she could tell, the guy had jumped into an ice cold shower.

That was actually a bit flattering.

He was totally naked. He'd even ditched those all-important gloves of his. The water crashed over him. His hands were flattened against the tiled wall, his head tilted down, and his shoulders hunched. He had some seriously broad shoulders—and he had a big, dark tattoo on his right shoulder. What was that, exactly?

She inched a bit closer to him as she tried to make out the design of that tat. The top looked like some kind of long, curving blade and—

Amber sucked in a sharp breath. It was a scythe.

Her lips parted. Okay. That was a little scary. But then, Cass was scarier.

He was also sexy. She should *not* find him sexy. She did. Sometimes, Amber thought she might be too much like Luke. Because she definitely had a dark side.

Cass's head turned. That bright stare pierced her through the glass.

"It's not helping." His voice was a low rumble.

She blinked. "Um, excuse me?"

He moved to fully face her and she realized exactly what wasn't being helped. The guy was aroused, most impressively aroused, and no, the cold water didn't seem to be helping his condition.

"I want you."

She could see that. But Amber spun on her heel, giving him her back. "Not happening, Reaper. Those hands of yours are bare, and if you think I'm in the mood for an up-close and personal dance with death, you need to think again."

In response, she just heard the water thundering down behind her.

Nervous, Amber kept talking. "Besides, if you're trying to woo a woman into your bed, kidnapping isn't a good first step. You probably should try flowers. Chocolate. Definitely chocolate. Not handcuffs. Save that stuff for later, you know? When you find out what kind of kink she likes."

The water kept pouring down.

Amber risked a glance back at him. His eyes were still on her. Her gaze dropped. *Oh, yes, definitely still turned on.* She swallowed. "I need to get out of here." And she stumbled forward but she just got a few inches past the door frame when she was jerked back.

Stupid invisible tie.

Bam.

"I am really hating you right now," she muttered. Being stuck to him via a five-foot tether sucked.

The water turned off. No more pounding. Just a steady *drip, drip, drip* of sound. She grabbed a towel and tossed it back at him without looking at his naked body.

"Don't worry, sweets. You aren't the only one who hates me. You're just another in the line."

His voice sounded—sad. Did the Reaper truly get sad? She looked back at him and saw that he'd wrapped the towel around his hips.

"I'm used to others fearing me—and hating me. That's nothing new."

Now she was feeling bad for him. "Cass—"

"We should get some sleep. We'll be heading out on a plane in a few hours."

Right. Because he still planned to turn her over to Luke and, yet, there she was, actually feeling *sorry* for the guy. Without another word, they headed out of the bathroom, and then he dropped the towel and climbed into bed.

She kept standing.

Cass patted the mattress next to him. "You can stand all night or you can sleep here."

Not a gentleman. "And you wonder why women aren't jumping into your hands."

But at least those hands were covered in gloves once more. She narrowed her eyes on the gloves in question. "Those will stay on all night, right?"

"Yes," he gritted out. "They will."

"Good. They'd better." Then she crawled over him and took the empty spot on the bed. He was under the covers so she made a point of staying on top of them. As soon as she dropped her head on the pillow, he turned out the lamp.

They were immediately plunged into darkness.

And she was far, far too aware of Cass lying next to her. She could practically feel him. He was warm and way too big and the guy took up more than his fair share of the mattress. If she moved just another inch, she'd be touching him. Not going to happen. Amber rolled away from him, giving the Reaper her back.

"Why does Luke want you?"

She should have known he'd get back to that. "I told you already, I took something of his."

"Maybe if you give it to me…maybe Luke will let you go. I can give whatever you took back to him, instead of trading you."

It's not that easy. "You're offering to let me go?"

Silence. He sure seemed to like silence.

"Thought so," Amber muttered as she punched her pillow. More silence. They were lying in bed, inches apart, and he was naked. They'd been having one hell of a make-out session before sanity had reasserted itself and he'd jumped into the shower.

What if sanity *hadn't* come back?

Amber knew she had to watch her bad boy weakness. It could *not* come into play again. Because the Reaper? She feared he'd take everything she had to give…and then he'd still turn his back on her in the end. Men couldn't be trusted. No one could be trusted.

Luke and Leo had taught her that long ago.

The clock on the bedside glowed at her, the bright digits seeming to mock her. Sleep had never seemed farther away. "So...you're a Reaper."

He moved in the bed, and the mattress dipped. Her body inched toward him.

"Yeah, I'm a Reaper."

"You...kill with a touch." She'd like to be clear on the rules regarding his power.

"It's one of the things I can do, yes."

She rolled toward him. Shock rocked through her. In the dark, his eyes glowed.

"I have a few more talents," he added in that deep rumbly voice of his.

I just bet you do. "The power is focused in your hands? I mean, other parts of your body can touch me—you kissed me—but it didn't hurt."

He stared at her.

"Just your hands," she said again. *Important point to know.*

"Just my hands. It's called the Death Touch for a reason."

Okay... "So why hasn't someone cut off your hands?" The question tumbled from her and she wanted to wince, but she didn't because they lived in the paranormal world. The kill or be killed world. And cutting off appendages? It happened with paranormals. It happened a lot.

She knew that from personal experience. Her shoulders seemed to burn.

"Someone did cut off my hands."

Her mouth seemed to go dry.

"I was six the first time they did it. I was tied up, and my hands were sliced right off."

Nausea burned in her stomach.

"But they grew back." He laughed—a dark, rough sound. Evil. "They always come back. You think my enemies haven't tried to stop my power? They can't. My hands regenerate. I'm the last of my kind, so that means I'm the most powerful. My enemies wanted to wipe out all of the Reapers, but they couldn't. I still fucking stand."

She found herself reaching out to him in the dark. *Another weakness I have.* Because she wasn't just evil on the inside. She wasn't just drawn to things that were bad.

She had this urge to—to help. To comfort. It was always there, eating away at her. Good and bad, opposites inside of her. One constantly fighting for supremacy over the other.

Amber touched his chest. *I was six the first time they did it.* "You must have been very afraid."

"You shouldn't touch me right now. The shower *didn't* help."

Her hand lingered on his chest. "You were only six..." He wouldn't have just been afraid. He would have been *terrified.* Amber wanted to keep comforting him, but her hand moved away.

Her fingers fisted. "What happened to the people who hurt you?"

"The same thing that always happens to those who come after me…I killed them."

She flinched.

"Go to sleep, Amber. You don't want to know anything else about my past."

"And I won't be around to see your future," she whispered.

They didn't have a future. She was his bounty, and soon he'd be dropping her off on Luke's doorstep. She shouldn't get involved with Cass. The less she knew about him, the better.

But…

Her eyes closed.

He'd just been six years old when they cut off his hands.

A tear slid down her cheek.

***

She'd…cried, for him.

Cass's gloved hand touched Amber's cheek, moving very carefully. She was asleep, so he'd moved closer to her. The tear track was nearly dry on her skin now. His index finger followed that faint line.

Strange. Cass didn't think anyone had ever cried for him.

Maybe the tear wasn't for me. Maybe she was crying because she's afraid. Because I'm taking her to the Lord of the Dark. A smart woman would cry when faced with him.

He eased away from her. Cass sat up in the bed.

She slept deeply, her breathing slow and easy.

He reached for the phone and dialed the concierge. So what if it was the middle of the night? The concierge was supposed to be twenty-four seven, right?

"How may I help you?" The voice on the other end of the line inquired in an oh-so-professional voice.

"I want flowers." His words were low and rasping. He didn't want to wake Amber. "Can you bring some damn flowers up here?"

"Uh, sir?"

"Roses." Those were popular, right? "Just bring some roses up here. Have them here by…" He stretched a bit, looking at the clock on Amber's side of the bed. "Four a.m." Because he planned to be out of that hotel by five.

"Sir, I don't think you understand—"

"I've got plenty of money," Cass cut in. "Just bring the damn flowers, okay?" He couldn't go out and get them, not without having to pull Amber with him.

She wanted flowers. He'd give her flowers.

"And put some chocolate in the vase, okay?" Cass snapped.

"In the vase…with the flowers?"

"Get the freaking things up here." He hung up the phone. Then he glanced at her, worried she'd woken. Worried she'd laugh at him for even trying—

She was still asleep. But…

A whimper came from her. Instantly, he was pulling her closer because she'd sounded scared.

In pain.

"It…hurts…" Her eyes didn't open. She burrowed closer against him, and he liked that.

But Cass didn't like the pain he heard in her voice.

Her head rubbed against his chest. "Make it…stop."

Amber talked in her sleep. Interesting.

"No one will hurt you," he said, and he found himself stroking her back. Trying to *soothe* her.

A Reaper, soothing. Ridiculous. Insane.

But his hand slipped over her back, rubbing up and down and gliding near her shoulder—

She let out a quick, pain-filled cry. "Make it…stop," she begged again, her voice barely a breath of sound. "Make it stop…Luke."

Cass stiffened. Then his fingers stroked her shoulder again. Her left shoulder. And he felt the faint edge of a raised scar beneath her t-shirt.

Anger pulsed inside of him.

His fingers slid straight across her back, moving to her right shoulder. Once more, he could feel the edge of a scar pressing up through the thin t-shirt.

"Luke..." Her breathing hitched. "I'm...sorry...please..."

Cass wanted to see those scars. He wanted to see just what pain had been inflicted on her beautiful body. He wanted to rip the shirt away.

Instead, he held her against him. He kept stroking her.

Soon she stopped whispering in her sleep. She stopped begging.

But the anger in him—it grew into a twisting rage.

Luke had hurt her before? Cass was sure the Lord of the Dark had hurt many, many people. He'd never really thought about the destruction and pain that had been created by Luke Thorne.

Yet...it mattered to him that Amber had been the one to suffer at Luke's hands.

It mattered a whole fucking lot.

CHAPTER SIX

Amber's eyes flew open and she jerked up in bed. The nightmare was fading, trickling away—a warning of the danger coming.

She hadn't been given a foreshadowing dream in a very, very long time. That meant some very serious shit was coming her way. Dammit. As if her luck wasn't already crap.

"You talk in your sleep."

Her jaw dropped as she swung her head toward Cass. Only Cass wasn't in bed with her. Fully dressed, he stood beside the bed, with his gloved hands on his hips. "You should warn a guy when you're going to get chatty in bed."

She closed her jaw—and jumped out of bed. "Not like I had a choice on sleeping with you!" But she had to focus on what mattered. "What...exactly did I say?" Because her head was aching from all the visions she'd had. Visions from her past. Visions from her present.

And, unfortunately, visions that could be from her future.

I have to get out of here. I have to run.

"Take off your shirt."

She huffed out a breath. "Did we not already talk about your seduction routine and how it needs way more work?"

A muscle flexed in his jaw. "I felt your scars."

He'd…Her hand lifted and she reached behind her left shoulder. Hell, you *could* feel the scars through her shirt. "When did you touch me?" She didn't remember that. They stood right beside each other and she glared up at him.

"I touched you…" And he touched her right then, reaching around to trace the scar beneath her shirt. "When you cried out in your sleep. When you pressed your body to mine and begged *Luke* to stop hurting you."

Her breath caught. He had details wrong. But…His voice had roughened. Anger? No, *rage* was there, bubbling just beneath the surface of Cass's words. "Let me get this straight…" She peered up at him. "You're about to hand me over to Luke on a silver platter, but you don't like the idea of him hurting me?"

His glittering gaze was answer enough for her.

*In that case…*She immediately spun around and yanked up her shirt. Amber tossed the t-shirt on the bed. "Take a good, long look." Normally, she hid her scars. They were ugly, twisting, the edges far too rough and tattered. But this wasn't a normal circumstance. She was fighting for her life. "See what he did to me."

His gloved hands touched her scars and—she felt a spark. A surge of heat that lanced right over the rough ridge of scars and into her body. A tremble shook her and she whirled toward him. She grabbed the gloves. "*What* are these made of?"

His face was hard with rage. "*What* did he do to you?"

She lifted the gloves up to her eyes, staring at them as her heart raced far, far too fast. "They're magic."

"They have to be, in order to hold back my power."

"*Very* powerful magic," she added, not caring that she was standing in front of him with her bra exposed.

His gaze dipped to her breasts. Heated. "Very powerful."

Dammit. "Did *Luke* give you those gloves?"

His gaze rose to meet hers. "Yes."

"I hate him."

Cass frowned. A sharp knock sounded at the door. She immediately tensed. "Leo!" Was that him at the door? He'd found them already?

"No, it's not him. It's room service. Or concierge—or some shit like that." Cass turned from her and headed for the door.

"Wait—you ordered room service?" That seemed so...normal. So not Reaper-like.

He was yanking open the door, she was standing there in her bra—so Amber gave a quick cry and yanked the shirt back on as fast as she could. But she hadn't needed to worry, he never let the guy at the door inside. Instead, Cass yanked a vase full of roses from the visitor and shoved a wad of bills at him.

"Thank you, sir, I—"

Cass slammed the door shut.

"That is so rude," she muttered as she hurriedly put on her shoes.

Cass stared down at the flowers. "They...are?"

"Not them. Roses aren't rude. Slamming the door is rude. You were supposed to thank him, and then nicely shut the door."

"I gave him money and I *did* shut the door." He paced toward her, the vase and those beautiful flowers held out in front of him.

"Yeah, but..." Her words trailed off. "Have you ever ordered room service before?"

"No." He had his arms fully extended and the vase was right in front of her.

She looked at the blood-red roses then up at his face, then back at the roses. She frowned. "Is that...chocolate in there?"

"It better be."

He was giving her chocolate and roses. He was holding the vase as if it were some sort of bomb, but the guy was actually giving her what she'd asked for…and despite everything, Amber found herself laughing. "Cass…is this your seduction routine?"

His cheeks heated. He glared at the roses. "You don't like them."

"I do, actually. Roses are my favorite."

His gaze shot back to her. The big, bad Reaper. He looked so uncertain as he held those flowers out to her. She started to take them from him, but then her gaze fell on the gloves once more. Such powerful magic.

Almost like the magic she'd once possessed.

Sadness slid through her. Goosebumps rose on her arms.

"Amber?"

Her breath whispered out as she confessed, "I may have lied to you—"

She didn't get to say anything else. The big window to her right suddenly exploded inward, sending chunks of glass flying toward her. Amber lifted her arms, instinctively trying to cover her face from the assault, but she knew it was useless. Too much glass. Too fast. Too—

Cass was in front of her. He grabbed her, pulling her face against his chest and shielding her with his body as that glass battered at them.

She could smell blood in the air—knew it had to be his—and she struggled to look up at him.

"Well, well…" A low, growling voice filled the room. "Look what I found."

That voice wasn't familiar to her. Not Luke. Not Leo.

Cass turned, still holding her tightly in his arms. An alarm was going off all around them—probably because the window had just exploded inward. And some guy—some guy with brown hair and dark eyes and a smirk on his face had just walked right out of the night and into their room.

He shattered the window. We're on the freaking fourteenth floor – the guy flew up here and shattered the window.

The stranger's smirk stretched and she saw his fangs. *Vampire.*

Cass's hold tightened on her. "Gregory."

"Holding out on me, old friend?" Gregory shook his head. "Because the word on the street is that you took another job for the Lord of the Dark."

This was bad. This was so bad. She tried to ease from Cass's grip. Her shoe crunched down on glass, but…not broken glass from the floor-to-ceiling window. Broken glass from the vase. It had shattered. Cass must have dropped it when he'd reached for her. The flowers had spilled onto the floor, and the roses looked like blood.

"Is she the bounty? She must be...Amber, I believe her name is. After a little persuasion, a friend down in New Orleans told me a bit about her."

Persuasion from a vampire generally meant he'd drained some poor fool and forced the guy to talk. Amber wondered who'd told this guy about her. Maybe one of her regulars at the bar?

"Gregory, get the fuck out of here before I stake your ass." Cass turned to confront the vamp, pushing her behind him and Amber had to gasp. There were at least a dozen shards of glass in his back. Big, thick shards.

They looked *so* painful. Her hand lifted and her fingers curled around the biggest chunk of glass—the one that was about an inch from his spine. She grabbed it and slowly pulled that chunk out. His blood soaked the glass and she tossed it to the floor. Then Amber reached for another piece.

"Cassius, you have an unfair advantage when it comes to bounty hunting. I mean, where's the danger when all you have to do is touch your prey in order to collect? Too easy. Hardly sporting of you."

"Gregory..."

"But when the prey has to be brought back *alive,* then things are different. That's the hard part for you, right, my friend?"

Cass gave a bitter laugh. "Is that what we are? Friends?"

She dropped another glass chunk to the floor and reached for a third.

"We used to be family," Gregory said. "We could be again."

Amber did a double-take. Cass's family included a vamp?

Gregory made a low, humming noise. "I'm guessing that pretty little piece behind you is one of those Bring-In-Alive bounties…or else she wouldn't still be standing. Tell you what…how about we split her bounty? I know Luke is the one who wants her, and I've been trying to get an in with him for quite some time."

The vamp wanted to get on Luke's good side? She dropped another piece of bloody glass. *What else is new?* Everyone always wanted to play nicely with the Lord of the Dark.

Everyone but her. She just wanted to stay away from Luke.

"You and I can both take her in. Amber…" Gregory seemed to taste her name. "Such a lovely bounty."

Cass took a lunging step forward. "I don't share bounties."

She peeked around at the vampire. His gaze dipped toward her. There was curiosity on his face—and anger. A cold, hard anger. His dark stare swung back to Cass. "Reaper, I'm asking nicely. I'm giving you a choice. We can be *partners* here..."

"I don't work with partners, and you know that, Gregory. Your sorry ass has been nipping at my tail for too long. You want to play in the big leagues? Fine, do it, but you won't get Luke's attention by stealing *my* prize."

She was a prize? So insulting. Amber glanced toward the door. She inched back a bit. She also kept her right hand curled around the last chunk of glass she'd taken out of Cass. It wasn't much of a weapon, but it was better than nothing.

"Did you follow me all the way from Key West?" Cass demanded. "From Key West to New Orleans? Then here? I thought I smelled some stench in the air. Had to figure it for the undead."

"Watch it," Gregory snarled. "I'm giving you a choice now. In about five seconds, there won't *be* a choice on the table. I'll be taking the pretty woman behind you, and I'll be Luke's new hunter."

"You're lucky I haven't killed you," Cass snapped back.

Yes...why hadn't Cass killed him? Was it that whole "family" thing that Gregory had mentioned?

"Five..." Gregory began. "Four..."

Wait—he was doing a countdown?

Cass took another step toward the vampire.

"Three..." Gregory snapped. "Two—"

"One," Cass fired right back. "Now get your ass *out*." Then he shoved his hands—*the gloves are gone!*—right at Gregory. Just like in the alley, a bright burst of light seemed to fly right from Cass's palms. That light hit Gregory and he went surging back. He fell out of the gaping hole that he'd created just moments before in the massive window and his body sank like a stone.

She ran to the window, peering down, and, sure enough, his body was a crumpled, bloody mess below. He'd hit the big statue that sat on the middle of the fountain near the hotel's entrance, and he looked…Amber swallowed. "I'm guessing that's a broken neck *and* back."

"And Gregory won't be down for long, so come on." He reached for her hand, but stopped when he saw she clutched a jagged chunk of glass. "Planning to use that on me?"

"When a vampire flies in a fourteenth floor window, a smart woman holds tight to any weapon she can find."

He shook his head. "Glass doesn't work so well against a vamp."

"It does if you use the glass to cut off a vamp's head." She gave him a grim smile. "Works great then."

"And you've cut off a vamp's head before?" Cass seemed doubting.

"Yes." He shouldn't doubt.

Surprise flashed on his face. Then Cass glanced back out the window. "He's starting to move. We have to *go.*" He reached out for the glass.

She yanked her hand back. "Your gloves!"

He immediately froze. "Fuck. *Fuck.* I didn't think—I could have—"

Could have killed me.

He spun and marched to retrieve the gloves he'd dropped on the floor. He also grabbed for her suitcase again. Good of him. She had a special prize in that bag that she'd truly hate to lose.

"Amber, let's get the hell out of here."

She glanced below. The wind rushed through that gaping window. The vampire *was* moving. *Definitely time to get the hell out of here.* She kept her glass and she followed the Reaper.

***

Humans were swarming around him.

"Suicide…can you believe it?"

"I saw the guy jump right out of the window…"

"Oh, God, I think he's still alive…"

Gregory's eyes opened. He couldn't move his legs, not yet, mostly because he was sure his spine was severed. Dammit. Cass could be such a bastard. A selfish bastard who wanted to keep all the glory to himself.

Too bad, asshole. Time for a new lead hunter. I've got plans for Amber…and for Luke. Plans that have been in the works for a very, very long time.

A woman scrambled toward him. Her eyes were wide and worried and the faintest odor of alcohol clung to her. "We're going to help you!"

Because he was still half-in the fountain, she had to slosh her way to his side. Gregory turned his head and realized the water around him had turned red.

Such a waste of blood.

"I'm a nurse," she said quickly. "I need you to lie still. You've got some serious wounds so please, don't try to make any sudden movements—"

His hand flew out and he grabbed her wrist. In the next breath, he'd yanked her against him and shoved his teeth in her throat.

That sudden enough for you, baby?

"What's he doing?" A man's voice barked out.

Getting my ass stronger, that's what.

Her hands fluttered against his chest. He kept drinking and the humans around him—they didn't even try to stop him.

That was the thing with humans. Emotions controlled them too much. Shock, fear. Horror. They didn't want to believe what they were seeing. And when they finally *did* believe…it was too late.

CHAPTER SEVEN

The *ding-ding-ding* of a winning slot machine filled the air. Their hotel lobby connected with the nearby casino, and Cass was using that connection to his advantage. He raced through the maze of slot machines and then cleared the blackjack tables. Gregory would need time to heal. The vamp would probably have to find a blood donor, too, so that gave Cass and Amber the lead they needed.

"Wait, dammit, just *wait!*" Amber dug in her heels.

Growling, he turned back toward her.

"Who *was* that guy?"

"Gregory."

She gave a quick little eye roll and muttered, "I got that part. I also got the vamp part."

"Then you know everything that's important. And we've wasted enough time." He pulled her forward and they rushed out of the emergency exit. They were in an alley, a dimly lit one, and he saw a motorcycle just waiting a few feet away. He pulled her toward the bike.

"Are you *stealing* that motorcycle?" Her voice was scandalized—and far too loud.

He looked down at the suitcase he'd lugged all the way from New Orleans. "That item you took from Luke…is it in here?"

Her lips clamped together.

Hell, maybe that was a yes. It was probably a yes. He took out the contents and shoved them into the saddle bags.

"Hey, be careful with that! That's everything I own!"

Then she didn't own much. And the thought pissed him off. He tossed away the suitcase and hopped on the motorcycle. Cass tried to figure out exactly how to hot-wire it. It had been at least five years since he'd had to hot-wire a Harley.

Amber didn't climb onto the bike with him. She just kept standing there, looking all scandalized. Given their current situation, he didn't think there was really a need for scandal.

Hello, I'm Death. And you're surprised that I steal because…? Cass sighed. "Newsflash, sweets. The other ride we were in happened to be stolen, too."

Her lips formed a little O.

"Now, we need to get our asses out of here. Gregory doesn't give up easily, and if the guy thinks he can take you, he is sure going to try."

She pushed his hands out of her way. "Let a professional work."

A profess—She was trying to hotwire the ride?

Less than thirty seconds later, the bike's engine growled. She gave him a satisfied smile. "I tinker. It's my thing."

That smile...the way her eyes lit up...*Gorgeous.* She rose and, not even thinking about it—his hand sank into the thickness of her hair. He pulled her head close to his and his lips locked on hers. The kiss was fast, hard, and not nearly deep enough. But that taste of her—that blend of honey and champagne—sent his blood boiling.

Reluctantly, his head lifted. His hand stayed in her hair. "Sorry about the roses," he rasped. "I'll get more. More chocolate, too."

Her eyes widened. Her lips were swollen and red and wet from his kiss. "Will that happen before...or *after* you turn me over to Luke?"

His jaw locked. "Get on the bike."

"Since you asked so nicely..." She climbed on behind him. He'd thought that he might need to tell her to hold tight, to urge her to move that delectable body closer to his.

But he didn't have to tell her anything. Her legs curled behind his, her breasts flattened to his back, and her arms locked around his stomach. "Haul ass, okay?" Amber urged him. "Because I don't exactly have a good track record with vampires."

His gloved hands curled around the handlebars. "So…you're a *human* who's managed to behead a vamp and piss off the two most powerful paranormals out there?"

She gave a faint cough. "What can I say? I have talent."

She had lies. And he didn't want them. He turned his head so that he could see her beautiful golden eyes. "You will tell me your secrets."

She smiled at him. "Only in your dreams."

His jaw locked. "Sweets, you don't want to know about my dreams."

"No." Sadness tinged her voice. "You don't want to know mine."

"Give her to me!"

The bellow came from the right.

Cass wasn't particularly surprised to see Gregory lunging out of the back exit and stalking toward them. Gregory never stayed down long. That was one of the things Cass had admired about the guy—back in the day.

Blood dripped down Gregory's chin. And he was dragging his back leg—that leg still looked broken.

"Someone's a fast healer," she muttered.

When someone had fresh blood, yes, he was. And Cass was betting that blood dripping down Gregory's mouth had come from a recent victim. "The Lord of the Dark doesn't like it when paranormals call attention to themselves!" Cass shouted the reminder at Gregory. "So Luke is going to be pissed if you've left a trail of bodies in your wake."

Gregory stopped. He lifted one hand and pointed at Amber. "I want her."

"Tell him that he's not getting me," Amber said, her lips moving close to Cass's ear.

Cass's lips almost twitched. "You're not getting—" he began.

"I want her!" Gregory bellowed.

"Over my dead body." And his lips weren't twitching any longer. Red hot fury filled him and he held out his right hand. Power pulsed, trailing from his tattoo to his hand, growing, surging...

"Um, what's happening?" Amber asked. Her hold on him tightened. "Because you just got a whole lot warmer."

Yes, he had. "I won't hurt you, just keep holding on."

He spun the motorcycle so that he was facing Gregory. Cass drove toward him, gaining speed. He knew the vamp would try to jump out of his way.

So he was bringing in a new weapon.

His scythe appeared in his right hand. He saw the fear flash on Gregory's face. Gregory had seen him use the scythe in the past, so the guy knew just how dangerous it was...particularly to a vamp.

Are you in the mood to lose your head? Because Cass was betting that Gregory wasn't.

"*Holy hell!*" Amber gasped.

The vampire was running, moving at his super human speed, so Cass threw the scythe, and it hurtled, tossing end over end in a fast arc, right to his prey. It sank into the vampire's back and Gregory fell to the ground.

Cass clamped both hands around the handlebars and turned the bike to the left. He didn't look back.

But Amber must have because she suddenly cried out, "That…that thing just vanished!"

Yes, the weapon would have vanished after it found its target.

"You have light that shoots from your hand, *and* a magical scythe? A tattoo that turns into a real weapon?"

"I have a few more tricks," he growled back at her. Maybe his words were a warning. And maybe he was just bragging because Amber had sounded impressed.

"Damn, Reaper, you are scary."

Yes, he was.

But she was still holding him tight. So maybe he wasn't too scary for her.

***

Fucking hell.

Gregory groaned as he pushed himself to his feet. Cass had actually used the scythe on him. Talk about hitting below the belt.

Or stabbing me in the damn back.

And to think…they'd once been best damn friends.

Friends always made for the most dangerous enemies.

He rubbed his back. The scythe would be gone now. He knew how that shit worked. Cass had that freaking magical tattoo on his back, and it let him call up the weapon whenever he wanted it. The weapon was his alone to command—another gift from Luke.

Talk about being the teacher's pet.

Gregory rolled his shoulders. His back *hurt.* He'd need even more blood now, but at least that blade hadn't severed his spine.

This time.

Once the scythe found its target, it vanished after impact. Very powerful magic. Magic that Cass shouldn't possess. He'd done a few favors for Luke and been rewarded too well.

I'll have those rewards. I'll be the one who sits at the devil's right hand.

Then…he'd be the one to take out the devil.

He could still hear the growl of the motorcycle, but he could barely stand, so chasing Cass and the mysterious Amber wasn't an option. Not then.

But I know how you think, Cass. You'll want the fastest mode of transportation. You'll want to fly away with your prize. Cass was heading back to Key West. Back to Luke.

I just have to stop you before you get there.

"Hey…buddy…you okay?"

A human male had just appeared to his right, clutching a garbage bag.

Gregory smiled at him. "Not yet, but I will be…" *After I take a bite.*

***

Cass drove fast and he drove hard and he took them away from the city and down a long stretch of dirt road that seemed to shoot into the middle of absolutely nowhere.

When Cass braked the bike, Amber knew her reckoning had come. She'd been trying to think of lies to tell him.

She'd just come up with jack.

As soon as the engine died, she jumped from the motorcycle. His hand flew out and locked around her wrist. "Going somewhere?"

"I wish," she mumbled, but then she notched up her chin. "I can't, remember? 'Cause you used some kind of mumbo jumbo magic on me, and now I'm practically chained to your side. *Not* cool, by the way. So incredibly not cool."

He stared at her. His blue eyes gleamed. "I want to know everything."

Trust me, you don't.

He shoved down the kickstand. "You aren't going to tell me, are you?"

"Tell you what?" She yanked her wrist free of his hold. "My life story? Sorry I don't feel like sharing with the man who has basically kidnapped me."

He rose and faced her. His arms crossed over his chest. "I would think you'd want to spin me some sympathetic story, maybe try to get me on your side so I won't hand you over to Luke."

Like she hadn't already considered that idea a dozen or so times. She glanced around the woods—they were dead silent. Almost eerily so. Amber swallowed. "Would that work? Would you really want the big, bad Lord of the Dark as your enemy because of me?"

He didn't answer.

She gave a bitter laugh. "I thought so. I mean—he'd destroy you. I get that you have to look out for your own life. Besides, if you made a deal with him, then you're bound to Luke. There isn't a choice for you."

A muscle jerked in his jaw. He hadn't liked her answer. Sometimes, the truth hurt. In this case, the truth had hurt them both.

"So you're just going to surrender to me now? Return to Luke like a good bounty?"

Her teeth ground together. "I'm not good. You shouldn't forget that. And, no, I'm not going back. I'll get away from you."

"No, you won't." Cass took a step toward her and he seemed to *surround* her. He was big and strong and his scent was oddly seductive. It was that danger-bad boy attraction again—her weakness. She was literally flirting with Death, and it made her feel alive.

Had Luke known? Had he realized she'd be drawn to her captor? Luke was such a schemer, always planning his moves so far in advance.

"Tell me what you took from him," Cass said.

"Are we back to this?" Her gaze dipped to his mouth.

"Tell me…or I'll find out on my own."

Doubtful.

The silence stretched between them. Too long.

"Fine," he gritted out, then he whirled and was grabbing for the saddle bags. He started yanking out the items—tossing her shirts, her underwear, her jeans.

"Stop it!" Frantic, she grabbed the clothes.

He didn't stop. A scarf was thrown next. Her *favorite* scarf. Then he was reaching for the black bag she'd actually hidden *inside* one of her shirts. He'd found that too easily. He opened the bag and pulled out a knife sheath.

Oh, hell.

He withdrew the knife from the sheath, and the bracelet she'd taken from him at the bar—that bracelet fell to the ground. For once, Amber didn't worry about her bracelet. Her gaze was on the knife. A real beauty of a knife. One with a gleaming blade and a big, thick emerald in the handle.

Cass gave a low whistle. "What were you going to do with this?"

She grabbed for it. "Give it to me!"

Instead of giving it to her, she found herself shoved beneath the stretching branches of a massive oak tree. Cass pinned her there with his body while one gloved hand gripped the knife. "I can feel the magic in this weapon. Very old, very potent magic." His eyes narrowed. "*This* is what you took from him?"

Her clothes had fallen from her hands, dropping back into the dirt. "That knife is *mine!* I didn't take it from Luke. That's not what he wants!"

His head dipped toward her. "I think you're lying to me again."

"No, not this time. That is *mine.* That emerald will buy me a new life." *Another* one. "I can trade it for a spell that will make sure Luke and Leo can't ever locate me. I just have to find the right wizard or witch and then I'm set—"

His eyes held hers. The knife was still gripped in his hand. "How many lies have you told me?"

Oh, shit. Shit. He didn't realize it, but he was holding a very, very powerful weapon that was known in certain circles as the Blade of Truth. When you held it, people near you were compelled to only speak the truth.

"A…lot," Amber heard herself mutter.

His eyes widened. "You're not human."

She laughed. "Hell, no." The words just fell out. Horrified, she slapped her hands over her mouth. She *had* to stop talking.

Cass blinked. "Then what are you?"

Her body shook as she tried to hold back the truth. She had to get that knife away from him.

"What. Are. You?"

Her hands fell back down to her side. Dammit. She'd *intended* to trade that oh-so-valuable weapon for her protection. She'd spent decades searching for the damn thing. And now—it was being used against her. How typical. "The last of my kind," she snapped at him.

Amber expected another hard question. What she didn't expect was the flash of raw sympathy that appeared on his face. "Me, too." He moved even closer to her. "Being alone…I didn't realize you were like me."

"I've been alone a very long time." Another truth.

Distract him. Take the weapon. Use it against him. If she didn't stop him soon, he'd learn every secret she possessed.

Her hands rose to flatten against his chest. She pushed up onto her tip-toes, and Amber put her mouth on his. He stiffened at the touch of her lips, and she thought he might pull away.

He didn't.

His lips parted. He kissed *her*. Deep and consuming. Hot and sexy. He kissed her with a raw skill and a desperate hunger that had her heart racing. She'd wanted to distract him…

Now she just wanted more of his mouth.

The kiss became even deeper. She wasn't just touching his chest, she was now moving her hands and clutching his shoulders. His left hand had curved around her hip and yanked her flush against his body. She could feel the long, thick length of his cock pushing against her.

A basic, undeniable truth…Cass wanted her.

And…her truth…She wanted him.

Wanting someone so much could be very dangerous. Especially when that someone was Cass.

Her eyes were tightly closed, her body leaned into him, and her hand reached for the knife that he still held. Her fingers slid over his, caressing, then she was curling her hand around the—

"Sweets…that isn't the move you want to make."

He'd lifted his mouth from hers. His bright gaze glared down at her—filled with fury and lust. "Don't play games with me. You won't win."

"I wasn't..." *Crap. He's still holding that knife.* So she couldn't stop her words. "I want you. I want you so much it scares me because I know you aren't a safe lover. You kill with a touch, and all I can think about is having you touch me everywhere."

His face changed. "Don't bullshit me."

If only. "I want you. I have...there is something inside of me that's...others have said it's wrong. That *I'm* wrong." She'd heard that accusation plenty of times. "I want the men I shouldn't. I want danger. I want darkness. I looked up in the bar and saw you and from the first glance, I wanted you."

"Then you found out I was the fucking boogeyman."

Her eyes squeezed shut, but she couldn't hold the words in. "And I still wanted you. Maybe even more." Because in her dark and twisted paranormal world, power was sexy. Cass had so much power within him.

"You...aren't lying."

Her lashes lifted. "No."

And then his face changed.

Shock...need...*lust*. Raw and wild and so savage. He threw the knife—just as he'd thrown the scythe before. It whirled and she heard the *thunk* when it sank into the nearby trunk of a tree. But she wasn't looking at that knife because Cass had locked both of his arms around her. He yanked her up against him and took her mouth. His control was gone—she could tell that immediately. His kiss was out of control, ferocious with its need, and her desire burst to the surface. She was as desperate as he was.

"It changes nothing," he growled.

The need. The hunger. "I know." The knife wasn't forcing her to share that truth. He wasn't touching the weapon any longer, but she was still telling him the truth. This time, the truth was her choice. Even if that truth hurt. Her hands wrapped around his neck and she pulled his mouth back to her.

She loved the way he kissed her. Loved the need and desire that she could taste. He kissed her with such intensity, as if she were the only thing that mattered to him.

He backed her up against that tree and his hand slid under her shirt. When she felt the touch of the glove on her skin, she jerked a little.

"Easy…I swear, I won't hurt you." Cass breathed those words against her mouth.

She believed him.

His hand slid up her rib cage. His mouth trailed down her throat. A moan slipped from her because he felt so good. She loved his mouth. She wanted it everywhere.

His fingers brushed against the edge of her bra. Her breasts were tight and aching and she—

A twig snapped. In a flash, Cass had yanked down her shirt and whirled away from her. His hands were fisted at his sides and he stared to the right, at a thick line of trees.

Her breath came too fast, too hard, and her heart was racing in her chest. Goosebumps were rising on her arms. She'd been too distracted to notice her alarm system going off. "It's…" *Not the vampire, don't be the vampire…* "Tell me it's not Gregory or Leo…"

"It's not." Cass didn't look back. His right hand lifted and she felt that odd hum of energy again…and then the scythe was in his hand. "*Show yourself!*" Cass yelled.

And the trees moved—no, something *burst* right out of the trees. A big, snarling black bear. Its fur seemed to explode from its body and it hurtled toward Cass.

Her jaw dropped.

"Ivan, turn your ass back into a human," Cass ordered, keeping the scythe at his side.

Less than two feet from Cass, the black bear halted. Its mouth opened and it let out a bellowing roar.

"Not impressed," Cass tossed back. "And you're about to lose some fur." He lifted the scythe. "I've had a seriously shitty day and it's barely dawn. Don't test me."

The bear...shifted. Slowly. Shifts were always brutal to watch. And to hear. Bones snapped and popped and the thick fur melted away until the beast was gone and a man stood in his place.

Ivan.

He rose—naked—and his gaze slid to her. He was tall, about Cass's height, but stockier with his muscles. His skin was a dark brown and his eyes were a sharp, contrasting green. Those eyes stared at Amber with curiosity.

Well, curiosity was better than a killing glare.

"I hate when you guys always wind up naked," Cass muttered. "Shifters...I swear, can't you cover your junk?"

Ivan tossed back his head and laughed. "Reaper, you are such a prude." He marched toward a nearby tree, and Amber averted her eyes. She thought it might be the polite thing to do.

"There, better?" Ivan called.

Her gaze jerked back to him. He'd put on a pair of sweats. The guy kept emergency sweats handy in those woods? If that was the case then...

Then they must be in the bear's territory.

Cass hadn't taken her down some random dirt road. He'd had a plan in mind. A destination.

Figured.

"I didn't mean to interrupt," Ivan drawled. The faintest hint of a southern accept dipped into his voice. "Thought you wanted a plane, but then I saw you and the lady and realized you were…you know, doing other things."

Making out. Getting hot. Yeah, other things. Feeling her face flame, Amber turned away from them and stalked to the nearby oak tree—not the one she'd been frantically kissing Cass under. The one that her knife was currently embedded in.

She yanked out the knife. The blade was slightly warm to the touch. Cass had been right. You could feel the weapon's magic.

"And what is *that* little trinket?" Ivan called out.

"Nothing for you to worry about." She put it back in the sheath and then hurriedly tucked the knife into her waistband—

"No." Cass was in front of her. He held out his hand. "I'll be taking that."

"It's *mine*."

"Is it? Or did you steal it from Luke?"

They'd already been over this. "Luke never owned this weapon. It's not what he's looking for, trust me, okay?"

Behind him, Ivan cleared his throat. Loudly. "Luke? Luke Thorne? I mean, that *is* who you're working for, right, Cass?"

Cass didn't look back at him. "How do I know you won't use that weapon to stab me?"

His question was just insulting. "I don't want you dead."

His lips curved. Uh, oh. That smile of his was absolutely devastating. "Good to know." Cass swiped the knife from her. "I'll just keep this safe for you, how about that?"

Her hands fisted. "I'm guessing I don't have a choice."

"You guessed right." He turned to face Ivan. "Is the plane ready?"

"Only if you want to come crashing to a quick and fiery death." Right after he said the words, Ivan's mouth dropped open. "What in the hell?"

Blade of Truth.

Cass stiffened. "You want to run that shit by me again? Because when we spoke last night, you promised me that you had a *fully* operational plane that I could use at dawn today."

Ivan raked a hand over his face. "You don't want to piss off a Reaper. If he asks for something, you say you have it." Again, he appeared horrified by his own words. "What in the hell is happening to me?" He paced toward them. His hand lifted and pointed one claw-tipped finger at Amber. "Are *you* doing this?"

She shook her head even as she asked, "Doing what?" Amber hoped she sounded innocent.

Ivan's eyes turned to slits. "You *are.*" He charged toward her.

Cass brought his gloved hand up and shoved it against the guy's chest.

Ivan immediately stilled.

"You don't hurt her. You don't even *think* of hurting her. I don't care how long we've known each other…you go at her, and we have a problem, got me?" Cass's low voice said the guy had *better* have him.

Ivan's stare had dropped to the gloved hand on his chest. He swallowed, and his Adam's apple bobbed. "I got you. And keep those freakin' gloves *on,* got me? I won't hurt your girl. I just—I had this thing all wrong. I thought she was the bounty…didn't realize the truth until I saw you two—shit, you know."

She knew. She also knew that she wasn't Cass's girl. But Cass didn't correct the bear shifter and neither did she.

"What's the problem with the plane?" Cass demanded.

"It's, um, I don't know." Ivan's eyes bulged as he said those words. "Fuck! Why is this happening?"

Cass tilted his head. His right hand still held the knife. His left hand pressed to Ivan's chest. "What, exactly, is happening?"

"I can't lie to you! That's what's happening!"

"Uh, Cass, we should really get going," Amber announced loudly. "Let me take a look at the plane. I bet I can fix it, no problem."

Now Ivan frowned at her. "You're a mechanic?"

"Absolutely." If that was what he wanted to call her, then she'd gladly accept that title. She was extremely handy when it came to mechanical work.

"It's an older Cessna, twin engine—"

"Got it." It didn't matter *what* the plane was—she could fix it. She could fix anything. That power had never left her. She hurried toward Ivan. Her hand slapped on his shoulder. "Come on. Let's go. Show me the plane. I'll get started and—"

"Amber."

She peered over her shoulder.

Cass's gaze darted from her to the sheathed knife. She knew he'd figured things out. "Why does Ivan have to tell me the truth?"

Dammit. "Because you're holding the Blade of Truth," she blurted.

"Fuck me," Ivan whispered. "I thought that was a myth."

She rolled one shoulder in a shrug. "Most myths are real. That's why life is fun."

He blinked at her. "Who are you, lady?"

He didn't have the Blade of Truth. She didn't have to tell him.

"How does the blade work?" Cass asked her.

She rocked back on her heels. "You hold it and you ask questions." She spoke too fast. "Anyone near you has to answer honestly. Lies just can't happen when the blade is close."

Cass glanced down at the sheath. "Interesting."

"Isn't it?" She slapped a smile on her face. "Now, in case you've forgotten—we have a vamp and a pissed off Lord of the Light on our trail. So how about I just get to work on this plane?" She nudged Ivan. "Show it to me."

"I haven't forgotten anything," Cass said.

Of course, he hadn't. And why had his words sounded like a warning?

But Ivan was turning to trudge back through the woods and she hurried to keep up with him. And since she moved—Cass had to keep up with her, too.

They were linked, bound still…until that forty-eight hours ended.

Maybe…maybe she could delay them…maybe she could *make* that forty-eight hours expire before he delivered her to Luke. If the forty-eight hours ended before Luke got her back, then she could have a chance to disappear.

Her head lowered as she began to plan.

CHAPTER EIGHT

"We're ready to fly," Amber announced. She was holding a wrench in her hand and a streak of dirt slid across her cheek. "She'll be good to go now."

Cass had to admit, he was impressed. He'd watched Amber and she'd seemed to know exactly what she was doing, no hesitations at all. She just jumped right to work on the small plane.

"Where did you train?" Ivan wanted to know as he gave a low whistle. "You've got that engine working like a dream."

She shrugged. "I didn't train anywhere. Or at least, not at any school or any place like that."

Ivan's jaw dropped.

"I just...I know how to make things work." She put down the wrench. "I've been putting things together and taking them apart for a very, very long time."

Cass stared at her. "You're sure this plane will fly?" He didn't have the knife in his hand—he'd already stowed it on the plane with a bit of gear and some back-up clothes that Ivan had given to him. At the earliest opportunity, though, he planned to take out that knife again. And to use it so that he could unravel all of Amber's secrets.

"I'm sure." Her stare met his unflinchingly. "But if you don't believe me, just ask your buddy here. He was watching me like a hawk."

Ivan nodded. "It's good." Then he turned and moved briskly toward the side of the plane. "Now you two need to get the hell out of here. This strip is off the radar for most folks, but I don't like to take chances, know what I mean?"

Cass knew *exactly* what he meant. He handed Ivan his payment and the cash vanished. "More will be wired to your account." Enough to cover the cost of the plane. He'd done business with Ivan plenty of times over the years. They had a standing agreement. "Thanks for the help, shifter."

Ivan glanced away, licking his lips. "Anytime, Reaper. Anytime." His gaze had darted to Amber. He was frowning.

Cass put his hands on his hips. "Is there a problem?"

Ivan raked a hand over his face. Amber was just a few feet away—as far as their invisible bond would let her go—and she was still peering at the front of the plane. "What is she? I mean...I swear, she smells human to me, and you know I have a good nose for things like that." His gaze slid back to Cass. "I don't like putting humans at risk." Because, once upon a time, Ivan had fallen in love with a human female. Unfortunately, she'd been caught in a paranormal battle—caught between bear shifters and vampires—and she'd vanished.

"She's not human." Cass was absolutely certain of that fact.

Ivan's shoulders relaxed.

"Gregory is after her."

The shifter took a step back. "What?"

"He tracked her down to the hotel we were staying at in Biloxi. The vamp thinks he can take her and start hunting for Luke."

"You…killed him?"

Cass lowered his voice. "No. I let the bastard keep living. After all, I owed him."

Ivan exhaled. "A lot of us owe him. Next to Luke, I'd say he's the paranormal who schemes the most. Always planning ahead. Always using everyone else…"

"His vampire clan took me in when I was a kid."

Cass heard the faint rustle of footsteps and saw Amber creeping closer, but he kept talking. Maybe she should hear this.

"Gregory's vampire clan took me in when I was at my worst. A fucking lost kid who'd been tortured for too long. I was more animal than human back then."

Amber gave a sharp inhale.

"They raised me. Taught me to fight. To hunt. To kill. Once, Gregory was the closest thing I had to family."

Her hands twisted in front of her. "The thing about family…they can turn on you, too. Sometimes, the worst danger that you can ever face can come from the ones closest to you."

He knew she was right. "Gregory and I can be too much alike." Again, he was warning her. "We hunted together for years, but he didn't like being second best. Now I guess he's ready to take over."

She licked her lips. "He's trying to take me."

Cass turned to face her. Ivan slipped away, moving toward the front of the plane and picking up the tools. "That's not happening. I don't give up a bounty to anyone." He moved even closer to her. "I'm not giving you up." The words came out rough and hard, but they were true. He wouldn't let her go.

"Except…to Luke. You'll give me up, then, won't you?"

His jaw clenched.

"I can't say anything to convince you to let me go?"

His chest burned.

"What is he giving you in return for me?"

He's giving me what I thought I wanted. Finally. But…Cass couldn't look away from her eyes.

And when he thought of his future, when he thought of a mate, he just thought of her.

"No answer, huh? Guess I should have used that Blade of Truth on you." She shook her head. "Whatever. I'm good enough to kiss, maybe good enough to fuck, but in the end, you'd still abandon me."

"No, I—"

She had already climbed into the plane.

Dammit.

Ivan cleared his throat. Cass glared at him.

The bear shifter held up his hands. "Easy, buddy. I'm on your side, remember?" He smiled, but the smile didn't reach his eyes. "You aren't thinking of letting her go, are you? Because if you went back on a deal with Luke…" He blew out a breath. "Hell on earth will have new meaning for you."

Cass didn't speak.

"Right. Okay, your funeral, then." Ivan pointed to the plane. "You still remember how to fly?"

"Fuck, yes."

"Then I guess I'll be seeing you." Ivan inclined his head. "Safe travels."

"Thanks." He climbed onto the plane. Made sure Amber was secure. Then he was in the pilot's seat, checking the instrument panel and buckling in.

"Didn't realize you would be our captain," Amber called. "What else can you do that I don't know about?"

Plenty.

He settled back into the seat and focused dead ahead. A few moments later, they were rushing down the makeshift runway and soaring into the sky.

Next stop…Key West.

And Luke.

Cass's chest burned once more. The next stop…would be the end of the line for him and Amber.

***

Amber sat in the front of the plane, her gaze on the land below them. Cass was at her side, flying as if he'd been doing it his whole life.

Every mile they took…it was a mile that brought her closer to Luke.

Closer to her past.

"He wanted you brought back alive," Cass's words were rasped. "Dead or alive…that's how I've brought in my prey before. Luke—sometimes he wants prey dead. And sometimes…sometimes he wants them alive."

Her gaze didn't waver from the ground. Everything looked small down there. "So he can make them suffer?" She didn't give Cass a chance to respond. "He has a prison on his island, you know. It's where he keeps the worst of the worst. Inescapable. If Luke locks you up, you don't get loose."

"He *doesn't* want you dead."

Her lips curled. "I know."

"I won't let him hurt you."

She had to laugh. "Do you really think you can stop him? Luke is the most powerful being I've ever met. He snaps his fingers and fire erupts. He blinks and people die."

"He hasn't faced a Reaper."

Goosebumps rose on her arms—and not because a threat was close. Her head turned.

The plane bounced a bit.

She stared at his hard profile. "Are you telling me that you can kill Luke?"

"A Reaper can kill any being that walks on the earth. Why do you think my kind was hunted so fiercely? Hunted, captured, our hands cut off right before we were killed..."

She had to swallow twice before she could speak. "You can kill Luke...and Leo?"

His head turned so that their eyes met. "I haven't put it to the test before."

So he didn't know but...*What if he can?*

"There wasn't a need to find out," he continued quietly. "Before."

The plane bounced again. Her hands flew out, gripping the arm rest.

"Turbulence," Cass said, not sounding even a little concerned. "Don't worry—"

But an alarm began to sound, a piercing shriek and the plane didn't just *bounce*...the nose tipped down and the plane seemed to drop.

He grabbed for the controls, yanking up hard. "What did you do?"

The ground was rushing up to meet them.

"You said you fixed the plane..." He was fighting and sweating and struggling to get the nose to rise—it wouldn't. *"What did you do?"*

She hadn't done *this.*

The plane kept shooting straight down. She could smell smoke. Could *see* smoke coming from the front of the plane. Dark, black smoke that shot into the air. The safety straps dug into her skin. "Cass?"

His face was locked in tight, angry lines. "We're fucking going down. We have seconds—*seconds!* Shit!"

She grabbed for his gloved hand and held tight. "Cass?"

His gaze held hers. The anger faded away. He stared at her...as if...

"Close your eyes, sweets," he whispered. "Everything will be okay."

No lie had ever sounded sweeter.

Her eyes closed. And then she felt his arms close around her. In that last moment, as she hurtled straight to her death, held tight in his arms, fear finally broke her.

Luke! Leo! Help me! Her mental call flew out even as the plane crashed down to the earth.

The plane shuddered, the smoke filled her nostrils, and Cass held her tight.

***

"They wouldn't have made it far," Ivan spoke quietly. Guilt twisted in his stomach as he stared at Gregory. He'd gotten the call from that vamp just moments before Cass and the woman had appeared in his woods. "I made sure of it."

Gregory smiled at him. "Considering what he is…Cass is far too trusting."

Yes, he was. Ivan had worked with Cass plenty of times over the years, and he *had* agreed to get Cass transport but…Gregory had something Ivan needed. Something he was desperate to have. "You have her? Vanessa is really alive?" The human he'd loved. The human who'd vanished during that terrible battle.

But Gregory had said that he'd saved her. That he'd transformed her and kept her close by.

Vampire, human, it didn't matter to Ivan what his love had become. He just wanted Vanessa back. He wanted her so much…that he'd just sent two people to their deaths. *I'm sorry, Cass.*

Gregory's smile stretched. "Of course…" He slapped his hand over Ivan's shoulder.

Hope burst in him, making him light-headed.

"…she's not alive," Gregory continued. He gave a low, rumbling laugh. "I drained that bitch years ago. She's rotting in the ground someplace."

Ivan's body went ice-cold. "But…but you said…"

"I lied." Then Gregory went right for his throat. Ivan tried to shove him back, but Gregory wasn't interested in drinking from him. The vampire used his fangs to slash Ivan's throat wide open. Blood sprayed into the air and Ivan fell onto the ground, his body jerking.

Gregory stood there, Ivan's blood dripping on him. "Everyone has a weakness," the vamp said. "She was always yours. If it makes you feel better…I don't think she felt pain at the end." That smile was on his bloody lips again. "I made sure she enjoyed her death."

Ivan tried to speak but couldn't. Too much of his throat was gone.

"Shifters are always most vulnerable in their human forms. For such a big, fierce bear, you sure did go down easy." He crouched beside Ivan. "Maybe you'll see your Vanessa in the next world, hmm? Then I'll have kept my promise and given her back to you." He dipped his finger in the blood that poured from Ivan's throat. "Or maybe not. I really don't give a shit." He rose. "Now…I have a crashed plane to find. I'm betting Luke will still pay me even if the bounty is dead on arrival. And I've got plans for Luke. I think it's time for someone else to be in charge, don't you?"

Ivan's body had grown cold.

Gregory walked away, not heading back for the road, but going to the small hangar that housed Ivan's other plane. The vamp knew how to fly, too. Once, he and Cass had flown together. Once, they'd been nearly best friends. But something had happened. Something that had made Cass turn away from the vampire.

Gregory would fly after the Reaper. He'd follow the smoke and flames.

Then Ivan knew he'd head for that final meeting with Luke. There would be no stopping him.

His eyes began to close. *Sorry…Reaper…*

***

Cass knew hell. He also knew heaven. He'd visited both, at different times.

The plane ignited and the fire swept back toward him. The crash was brutal, jarring, and he held as tightly to Amber as he could. They both went flying on impact, but he didn't let her go.

He wished he'd said more to her, wished he'd learned all her truths...

But there had been no time.

Death was brutal. Fast and hard. His body burned with the agony, but it was one he'd felt before. He was the last Reaper...and that meant something.

It meant he could never stay dead. All of the power of his people—it had come to him. As the others had died out, as they'd been slaughtered, their powers had drained to him, coming in like a beacon.

He hadn't even realized it. Not until the first time he'd been killed.

Back when he'd been six.

He died, but he didn't stay dead. Heaven, hell—neither could keep a strong hold on him. A Reaper always had to walk the earth.

And he was the last one. *He* had to walk.

He had to rise.

So he came back, his mouth opening and a roar of rage escaping him. He came back—this time from hell, from the pain and the horror, and he opened his eyes to see more fire around him.

And to see Amber...held in his arms, but still. So still...

He was afraid then. Terrified beyond his darkest dreams. He put his hands on her chest—the gloves still covering his fingers—and he fought to bring her back. He pushed on her chest, again and again. He breathed for her. He begged her…

Come back. Come back.

Another breath.

Don't leave.

He pushed on her chest.

Stay with me…

CHAPTER NINE

"You will *not* die."

Something hard pressed on to her chest. Amber tried to get a breath but couldn't and then—

Air. Air was filling her lungs. Power pulsed in her body. Her eyes opened.

Cass stared down at her. A deep gash was on his forehead, bleeding too much, and he stared at her with glittering eyes. With…

Fear?

"Fuck, yes," he whispered. "You came back." Then he yanked her into his arms. He held her tight, so tight that her bones ached, but she didn't care. He was warm and strong and they were both *alive*.

Though she seriously had no clue about just how they'd survived. The last thing she remembered was him telling her to close her eyes. He'd pulled her close and then…

Oh, no. I called for Luke and Leo. She pushed against him. "We…we have to go."

His mouth crashed onto hers. He kissed her with desperation and need and a dark desire that pulled at her very soul.

She wanted to keep kissing him back. But…they had some seriously big problems to deal with right then. Amber pulled her mouth from his. *"We have to go!"*

He tensed. His head lifted. His gaze was burning as he stared at her.

Burning…

Her nostrils flared as she became aware of the smoke and flames around her. Her head turned and she saw that they were in the middle of the wreckage. Chunks of the plane were on fire. Glass was everywhere. Fire. Hell.

"How did we survive?" They shouldn't have. No way should they have made it.

"I'm Death," he said simply.

She turned back to look at him, her heart tight in her chest.

"I'm Death and I have to walk the earth. One way or another…"

That was scary and she wasn't even exactly sure what that meant.

"I tried to protect you from the impact. I knew I'd come back…it was you that wouldn't." His eyes glittered. "And you were so still. You weren't breathing. I know death, but I don't know life. And you needed *life.*"

He rose, and he lifted her up, holding her in his arms.

She could have walked, maybe. She wasn't exactly sure of what injuries she had. Amber was a bit too stunned to take stock of things. "Why didn't you die?" Amber whispered. That whole *"I'd come back"* part nagged at her.

"Who says I didn't?"

What?

His hold tightened on her and he started walking away from the wreckage. Heading toward the line of trees. They seemed to have crashed near the edge of a swamp, and the twisting cypress trees were all around them.

Had he died? Had she? She didn't want riddles, she wanted the truth and—

"The knife!" She grabbed for his shirt front. "I have to get the knife. I *need* it!"

"I already have it, sweets. I strapped it to my leg right after I boarded the plane."

He'd…what? She didn't remember seeing him do that. *Sneaky Reaper.*

"That was how I knew you hadn't sabotaged the plane. Ivan did it. The bastard set us both up to die."

"Why would he do that?"

"I worked with Ivan in the past…and Gregory worked with him, too."

Gregory. Her new least favorite vampire.

"I'm guessing Gregory got to Ivan. Made him an offer too good to pass up." His jaw hardened even more. "So that means that fucking Gregory will be closing in on us."

"He's the least of our troubles." At the moment. *Luke and Leo are both coming here…because I called out to them.* She and Cass had to haul ass—seriously fast. But how?

He kept walking. Kept carrying her. There were no cars, no motorcycles. No boats. *Nothing.* It looked as if they'd crashed into the middle of absolutely nowhere.

"It's going to be okay," Cass told her. "I'm going to keep you safe. You don't have anything to fear any longer."

"We both have plenty to fear, trust me," she muttered.

"I won't give you back to Luke."

Her eyes widened.

"I can't." He stopped walking to stare down at her. "I can't let you go. I'll do *anything* to keep you with me."

"Cass?" Something had changed between them—she could see it in the way he looked at her.

"I'd never been that scared. You weren't breathing. I've seen so many people die. *Thousands.* You were…you *are* different. The world can't keep going unless you're in it." His jaw hardened. "Not *my* world."

Then he was walking again, carrying her through the woods and she curled her arm around his neck. "You…you protected me." She was trying to piece the last moments of that crash together. She'd been surrounded by him, held so tightly in his embrace. "What did you do…make yourself my air bag?"

He gave a rough laugh that rumbled against her. "Something like that. I knew I'd come back, so the trick was making sure you survived."

And she had.

"But then you weren't breathing."

"So you breathed for me," she whispered.

He smiled. Had she ever noticed just how sexy his smile was? "Seemed a simple enough price to pay to make sure you stayed in this world."

Tears stung her eyes. He didn't get it. "Luke and Leo will come. And they *will* take me from you." He should leave her. He should get the hell away. Luke wouldn't handle a betrayal well. She knew that from past experience. And if Cass was really going to stand between her and the Lord of the Dark…

It's what I wanted. But I can't let Cass suffer for me.

Because something had changed for her, too. When a man died for you, it changed everything.

"They can try." He didn't seem worried. His steps didn't falter. "But I've finally got something worth fighting for."

And her heart warmed.

She rested her head against his chest. Her whole body ached, but she was a fast healer—another left-over trait from a time long gone. It was also damn hard for her to die—most days. She doubted a human would have walked away from that crash—or even been carried away—alive. But thanks to Cass and her own genetics, she'd survived.

Now what?

They made it to a road. A small country road. She didn't know if they were in Mississippi or Alabama or Florida. She just knew Cass was covered in blood, testimony to the injuries he'd taken for her—and he was holding her so carefully in his arms.

"Lift up your thumb, sweets," Cass murmured to her. "Help is on the way."

She didn't hear—

The rumble of a truck's engine reached her ears just as she saw the vehicle round the curve on the narrow road. Cass had better hearing than she did. The man just kept surprising her.

Supernatural tricks.

She lifted her thumb. "He's not going to stop."

Cass walked into the middle of the road. "I won't give him a choice."

She turned her head to stare at the truck that was fast approaching them. The last thing she wanted was a head-to-head impact after the plane crash and if that truck didn't slow…

"Smile, sweets. No one can resist your smile."

She smiled, knowing that what Cass was saying was utter bullshit.

But the truck stopped. Probably because a blood-covered man was in the middle of the road, clutching a stunned-looking woman. *Not* because of her smile.

"What happened?" An older man with grizzled cheeks and white hair hopped out of the truck. "I saw that cloud of dark smoke and thought someone needed help!"

Ah, the cloud of dark smoke…from their plane crash. Right. She was sure the crash would be creating all sorts of trouble. Human authorities would swarm soon to the scene.

"We need a ride," Cass said. "We're gonna need that truck."

The old man blinked. "What?"

Her gut clenched. She put her lips near Cass's ear. "Do *not* kill that man."

Cass's head turned. His lips brushed hers. "I was going to pay him."

Oh. Awesome.

He looked back at the man. "How much? For the truck…and to forget you ever saw us?"

Wait…was Cass forgetting that they had nothing on them? They'd just left a plane crash for goodness sake!

"Five grand," the driver spit out, looking shocked that he'd even made that statement.

"Give me your name and your address."

"J-John Parker. I live at 5808 Glendale…"

"Start walking, John. I'll see that you get the money."

John's face reddened. "You think I'm leaving you with my truck? Oh, *hell,* no."

Cass sighed. Then he sat Amber down on her feet. Before she could even blink, he had his scythe in his hand.

And the human was backing away—fast. Not just backing away—running. Running down the road so fast she would have thought he was a kid.

"Guess that means we get the truck." Cass looked back at her. "But don't worry, I'll send him the money. I'm a man of my word."

Or he had been. But if he was really going to betray Luke…

She glanced back at the dark smoke billowing in the air. "How fast do you think that truck can go?"

"Let's find out…"

***

Luke Thorne slammed down into the middle of the wreckage, his heart racing and a scream still echoing in his ears. "*Amber!*"

The still flickering flames vanished in an instant but the thick, black smoke kept billowing. He rushed to the left, to the right, searching those twisted chunks of metal. Fear was an acid in his throat. Fear...he *hated* fear.

Luke! Leo! Amber's voice had been in his mind, her terror so real that it still flooded him.

"What did you do?"

Luke stiffened. He knew that voice—it could have been his own voice. He turned.

His voice. His face.

His twin.

"Where is Amber?" Leo's wings were out, the scales seeming to glow. Fury had twisted his face. "What did you do to her?"

"Nothing." Why was he always the bad guy? *Oh, wait...*

Leo grabbed him, his fingers digging deep into Luke's shoulders—not fingers, but claws. When Leo's emotions got the better of him, his true form often emerged. "I know you hired the Reaper to find her. Why? You were supposed to let her go! We *both* were!"

"I changed my mind."

Leo threw him into the air and Luke slammed into what he *thought* might have been the plane's wing.

"Is she dead?" Leo's voice was quieter now. And with the Lord of the Light, quiet was a danger signal.

Just as it was for Luke.

Luke took a slow, deep breath and rose to his full height. His wings weren't out. Neither were his claws. Yet.

Leo looked away from him. "She always chose you. Why the hell would she do that? You were *worthless.* You guarded the dark. The monsters. She didn't need them. She needed—"

"You?" Luke tossed back. It was an old argument. "You with your judgement and your coldness? You kept everyone away, you still do. You think you know what's best. That only you can say what's right, but believe me on this, brother…you're wrong."

Leo's hands had fisted. Because his claws were still out…blood dripped from those fists. Leo had shoved his claws deep into his own palms. That was an old habit, one that only Luke knew about.

Leo hurt himself when bad things happened—sometimes, it was the only way he could feel.

"She is light and she is dark. Amber always was. And that was what ripped her from us both." Luke eased out a slow breath. "But no, to get back to your question, she's not dead."

Hope flashed on Leo's face, and, for a moment, Luke remembered when they'd been children...before the world had said that...one day...one twin would kill the other.

That day hadn't come. Not yet.

Leo kept ruling the so-called "good" paranormals.

And Luke ruled the "dark."

"How do you know she's not dead?" Leo rasped.

"Because I hired the Reaper. And I told him that she had to be brought to me *alive*. He hasn't failed me before. He *won't* fail me now." Luke nodded. "He has her."

"Then summon him! Get that bastard here!"

Unfortunately, things didn't work that way—at least not with the Reaper. Luke couldn't control him. *Another deal, long ago*. But he didn't reveal that truth to Leo. Instead, he said, "Summon him? Why? So you can try and take her away from me? Try and convince her—once more—that she should fear me? Hate me?"

Leo stared him straight in the eye. "She should. She should fear you. She should hate you." His shoulders sagged. "Just as she should hate me."

Because they both knew the truth.

"We will destroy her," Leo whispered.

And, one day…each other.

"Sometimes," Luke said as he tipped back his head and glared up at the black smoke. "I fucking hate prophesies."

CHAPTER TEN

"Summon the fucking hunter," Leo snarled.

His twin was always so impatient. Didn't he get that was a major character flaw? One of many that Leo possessed?

"Stop jerking me around. He's one of yours, so call him."

Luke sighed. "Yes, the Reaper *is* one of mine." Which meant he should be able to control the bastard. But...*Doesn't work that way.* So instead of a big confession about how he'd made a previous deal—or a *few* previous deals with the Reaper, Luke lied. He was good at lying. "I think her magic is affecting him."

Leo stood in the middle of that wreckage. "What?"

"I suspected it would happen when I sent him after her." Luke tapped his chin. "Only to be expected really. I mean, she paid for magic to hide herself from us."

Leo growled. "Tell me something I don't know."

There's plenty you don't know, brother. "We can't find her unless we're ten feet in front of her. That's the spell she crafted." He'd learned that after a lot of careful research. "Well, since the hunter is *with* her now, her magic is acting like an umbrella, covering him, too. When he's near her, I can't see him, either. She cloaks him." Luke thought that sounded like a good enough excuse. Better than…*So, yeah, once upon a time, I gave him a few magical upgrades.*

Leo began to pace. "I *had* her, in New Orleans. Couldn't believe my eyes. It had been so long. And he stood there, putting himself between us. He was so determined to get her back to *you.*"

Luke nodded, satisfied. "And he *will* bring her to me. I'm betting Cass has no idea that Amber called out to us. If she hadn't been scared as all hell, she wouldn't have." And that pissed him off. He'd told the Reaper to take care with her. Amber should have known no fear. "But she's okay. He has her, I'm sure of it. And he *will* complete the mission for me."

"You don't know that." Leo turned and paced to the left. "He could walk away from you. If he stays with her…hell, you'll never be able to control him. They could go anywhere."

"He won't do that." Luke crossed his arms over his chest. "Have a little faith, would you?"

That got to Leo, just as Luke had known the taunt would. Leo surged toward Luke. "What makes you so *sure?*"

"Because I promised him the thing that he wants most in the world. And he *will* trade Amber to get that."

"What? What do you have?"

Luke smiled grimly. "Someone he can touch, with his own hands. Someone who won't be afraid of his monster. He wants a mate, and he made a deal with me. He won't go back on that deal."

But Leo's eyelids flickered. "Love? Is that what this is about?"

"It's about a great many things…" He looked up at the sky. "That plane up there has been circling us for a quite a while now. You know what I want to do? I want to find out who's spying on me." So he spread his wings, let them shoot out of his back, and then Luke flew straight up into the air. He reached the plane in seconds and saw a familiar figure inside.

Gregory? Gregory Cethin? Why in the hell was the vamp circling him like a vulture? Luke ripped open the small door and wind whipped inside the plane.

"*Luke?*" Fear shook Gregory's voice. "Wh-what are you doing here?"

Luke's wings flapped. "I was going to ask you the same thing…"

***

"I need to shower off the blood." They were in some no-tell motel, after having driven hell fast for hours. They'd made it to Florida, and taken refuge in the first quiet spot they'd found. Cass knew they wouldn't have long to rest, and he was fucking sick of having his own blood soaking his clothes. His body had healed completely, but the blood still stained his skin and garments. Trying to keep his voice soft, he said, "Why don't you just rest a bit on the bed?"

Her lips quirked. "Sorry, but I think that bed is more than five feet from the shower."

Shit. The magical link. "Amber…"

"I want to shower off, too," she said, tilting back her head and the thick mass of her hair slid over her shoulders. "Think it will be big enough for two?"

He stopped. Just—stopped breathing. His heart stopped beating. Everything in him just stopped for a moment.

"Unless…that's a problem for you?"

Fuck me. His heart raced in a double-time rhythm, his breath came too fast, and his cock shoved against the front of his jeans. "Not a problem." Not at all. "I can wear the gloves. I can keep my hands off you—"

"Do I have to keep my hands off you?"

He took a step toward her, then caught himself. His control was razor thin. *Razor.* Did she have any idea…any clue how much he wanted her in that moment? "You know what I am…" His voice was too rough.

"I know who you are."

Who, not what.

He frowned at her. "You…you want to touch me?"

"I want to touch every single inch of you." She licked her lips. "You know I want you."

He was going mad for her.

"So can I come into the shower with you? How many times does a lady have to ask?"

A lady had *never* asked him before. Didn't she get that? Women—even those who'd come to his bed—had been afraid. They'd barely touched him at all. They'd just wanted the dark thrill of saying they'd fucked Death.

Vampires had enjoyed that particular thrill. Vampire females could be fierce and demanding. Their desires so dark…

She isn't like them. He still didn't know just what kind of paranormal she was. And he… "I'll be careful with you," he promised her.

Her full lips curled. "I know."

He lifted her into his arms. She seemed so light. She *fit* against him, or at least, she seemed to.

"You don't have to carry me, you know. The bathroom is like ten feet away."

He liked holding her. She didn't understand just how starved he'd always been for physical contact. And when he touched her, Amber didn't flinch away. She didn't look at him as if he were a freak.

He put her down on the bathroom tile. He turned on the shower, making sure to get warm water pouring out for them. The shower was small, and it was going to be a tight fit—and he didn't care.

Amber, naked in the shower, touching him?

Fuck, yes.

His hands reached for her shirt, but he caught himself and stopped.

"Cass?"

He cleared his throat. "Do you want me to…take off your clothes?"

"That depends…do I get to take off yours?"

He grabbed for the counter and held it so tightly he thought it might shatter. That razor thin control? *Nearly gone.* He wanted to rip her clothes away. Wanted to put his mouth all over her.

He wanted to see her face when she came for him. How much pleasure could she stand? He was ready to find out.

"I'll take that as a yes." She reached for him. Her fingers curled around the bottom of his shirt and she pushed it up. He grabbed for the fabric and nearly ripped it off as he jerked it over his head and dropped it to the floor. Her hands pressed to his abdomen and then her nails were raking down…down to the snap of his jeans.

Cass sucked in a sharp breath as she popped that button free. Then she slid down the zipper.

He grabbed her hands. "Sweets, you are about to drive me right over the edge."

She rose onto her toes. She nipped his lower lip. "Good."

Fuck…

He grabbed the hem of her shirt and she helped him to toss it aside. She'd already kicked off her shoes, so it was easy to get her jeans off and to throw those aside, too. When he saw her in her bra and panties, he just wanted to take a second to admire her, but his dick was aching and hard and he just had to touch her—

His shaking fingers slid under her bra strap. He still had on the gloves. He wouldn't risk her, not ever. He hoped she understood that.

"You're being so careful." Her long lashes swept down to cover her eyes.

Yes, he was. He could show her that he wasn't just some monster—

Amber licked her lips. Her lashes rose. "Don't remember asking for that." Then she unhooked her bra and tossed it *at* him. Her hands went to her panties, and she pushed them down her perfect legs.

He reached for her, but she'd slipped into the shower. Amber lifted her hand and crooked her finger toward him. "What are you waiting for?"

Nothing. He stripped, making sure to carefully unstrap the knife's sheath from his ankle. He put the knife on the floor and stalked into the shower. Her back pressed to the tiled wall and his hands slammed against the tile on either side of her head. His mouth took hers. Hard and deep and her taste just drove him even wilder. He wanted her. *All* of her. Her breasts pressed against his chest. Her nipples were tight, hard, and he just had to taste…

His hands moved to her hips. He lifted her up, holding her easily, and he brought her breast to his mouth. His tongue curled over the nipple, and she moaned. He took that nipple into his mouth, sucking deep, and she gasped. Her hands locked around his shoulders. Her nails bit into him.

He sucked her harder. He sucked her deeper. He kissed, he licked, and her moans were making him frantic. Cass kissed a path to her other breast, then gave it the same sensual attention. The water pounded down and he didn't care.

He needed Amber. Needed *in* her. And there could be no more waiting.

"Wrap your legs around me." The words came out guttural.

She locked those silken legs around him. His cock pressed to the entrance of her body. She was so hot. So…

Amber arched against him, taking his cock deep inside.

So hot. So tight. So perfect.

For a moment, he couldn't even breathe. And that control that had been sliced so thin? It vanished.

He pinned her to the shower wall, kept her legs locked around his hips, and he thrust into her, pounding hard again and again. Her head tipped back against the wall, and he kissed her throat. He sucked the skin, then bit lightly.

"Cass!"

His gloved hand was between their bodies. He stroked her clit, needing her to be as wild as he was.

Her nails clawed at him.

She is as wild.

Her hips slammed against his. They were fighting for their pleasure, neither of them holding back. She was the sexiest thing he'd ever seen.

Want all of her. Will take everything.

He felt her sex contract around him and her face went slack with pleasure. Her eyes burned at him as she choked out his name.

He kept driving into her, the pleasure so close. But he hated for it to end. He wanted to freeze that moment. Wanted to keep fucking her forever because nothing in his life had ever felt this good. This right.

This perfect.

But then the pleasure hit. It slammed into him and the whole world seemed to go dark for an instant. His body shuddered, his heart thundered, and the climax reverberated through every cell in his body. The pleasure ripped him open—he couldn't breathe it was so intense. He could just hold on for the fucking best ride of his life.

CHAPTER ELEVEN

Slowly, Cass withdrew from Amber's body. He lowered her legs back to the shower floor. The water was still pounding down.

Amber slipped past him and let the water wash over her. When she moved, her back was to him, and his gaze fell on her scars.

His hands lifted and he touched those scars, two round scars on each shoulder blade. She stiffened beneath his gloves.

"When you touch them, I feel a warmth." She looked back at him. "Heat. Like magic pouring into me." Her gaze seemed so dark and deep. "Do you know…what are those gloves made out of?"

He didn't know. "Luke gave me the gloves. I'm not even sure what all magic he put into them. I just…I needed to touch without killing."

Her gaze held his. "And what did Luke require for this little gift?"

"Four bounties."

"Alive…or dead?"

His hands fell away from her back. "Dead. They were…they were vampires who'd gone rogue. They'd found a way to resist Luke's powers and they were trying to rebel against him. He was furious—wanted blood. Nothing would stop him from having their heads." Fucking literally.

Her face paled. "Four vampires…"

"That was when Gregory turned against me. He said I shouldn't hunt his kind. But those *weren't* the same vampires who'd taken me in. They were sadistic bastards who were torturing humans. Led by a vampire werewolf hybrid named Hycim, they left blood everywhere they went."

"Yes, they did."

She *knew* them?

But Amber turned away and put her face beneath the spray of water. He wanted to touch her again, but he could feel that something was wrong.

Then she stepped out of the shower. Amber reached for a towel and dried off quickly. He moved beneath the spray of water, but he kept his gaze on her.

Something is very wrong. Moments before, everything had seemed so very right. "You…you did know Hycim, didn't you?"

She wrapped the towel around her body. "He cut off my wings."

What? Cass's hand flew out and he yanked off the water.

"I'm sure you realized that I once had wings. My scars are very specific, wouldn't you say?" Her smile was sad. "Hycim was incredibly strong, and he enjoyed using the darkest of magic. That magic helped him to resist Luke. He actually wanted to *kill* Luke, you see. And he managed to catch Luke at a vulnerable moment."

"Hard to imagine Luke vulnerable."

"Because he's not that way often."

His hands fisted and he remembered Hycim. The guy had been six foot five and thick with muscles. The only vampire/werewolf being in existence, he'd been heavy with power.

"Hycim cut off my wings with his claws. A normal weapon never would have taken them from me." She bit her lower lip. "But...truth be told, I agreed to give Hycim those wings. They were a trade. He was going to give me something I wanted in return for them."

"What did you want?"

Her head tilted to the right. "What do *you* want, Cass? What deal did you make with Luke? You tell me your terms and I'll tell you mine."

I was going to trade you for another woman. For a mate I could touch. For some reason, he just couldn't force those words out. Maybe because...because he knew they would hurt Amber, and he didn't want her hurt.

"I traded for someone I cared about," she said softly and he saw her shoulders sag, as if she'd given up on getting an answer from him. As if she knew wanting that answer was pointless. "He needed time to get his strength back…he just needed time, and my wings gave him that time."

Jealousy burned through him. She'd sacrificed her wings for some dumb bastard out there?

"The wings seemed like a small price to pay but…I didn't realize the consequences. For me. For him. For everyone." She swallowed. "When Luke sent you after Hycim…did he ask for you to…to make him suffer?"

He had. Luke had been very specific about the pain he wanted Hycim to endure.

Her eyes squeezed shut. "Don't…don't say anything else, okay? I just…" She spun around and hurried from the bathroom.

Cass didn't bother drying off. When she moved, he moved—they were still bound. Tied on a damn invisible string. Only he found that he didn't mind that connection. He actually dreaded the moment when their bond would vanish. What would happen then?

Would she slip away from him?

Was he supposed to just let her go?

She stood at the foot of the bed. Her towel dipped below her shoulder blades, so he could see her scars. He could touch them. And he did…but not with his hands.

With his mouth.

His lips pressed to the scar on her left shoulder. "I'm sorry he took your wings." And Cass actually wished that he could kill Hycim all over again. Because it must have hurt her, so much, the agony must have ripped right through her when the bastard had used his claws on her.

Cass had seen the carnage left when Hycim was done with his victims. That had been one of the reasons he'd taken the job from Luke.

Another reason…

The gloves. The fucking gloves.

His mouth moved to her right shoulder. Tenderly, he kissed that scar, too.

She turned in his arms. Tears swam in her eyes. For an instant, Cass could have sworn that his heart actually stopped as he stared at her.

"Take off the gloves," she said, her voice husky.

But Cass shook his head. "I can't." *You'll die.*

"Don't touch me with your hands. You can do that, right? If I ask you not to touch me, I can count on you. I can trust you."

Trust.

He'd gone still. "Are you sure you know what you're asking?"

"I'm asking you to take off the damn gloves." She swiped her hand across her cheek, catching the tears that had fallen. "Then I want you to get on the bed. Wrap your hands around the headboard."

His gaze shot to the headboard. It was wooden—made of two long slats. If she wanted him to grab the headboard, then he could spread out on the bed and wrap his hands around that bottom slat.

"Hold tight to it. Don't let go. I want to be with you again. But…I want it to just be us."

She was walking down a very dangerous path. Amber talked about trust but… "My control is too weak with you. I'm afraid I'll hurt you."

The Reaper…afraid.

She smiled and he was pretty sure his heart broke. "It's *because* you're afraid that you won't. Somewhere in that dark heart of yours, you aren't as bad as you want the world to think." Her lips twisted. "Or as Luke might want you to think."

"No." She was wrong on that. "I am bad, Amber. I've killed more people than you can imagine—and I'll kill more. Death is what I was made to do. I'm not human. Wouldn't *want* to be. I enjoy the power." He wouldn't lie. "You think I didn't go after the beings who'd killed *my* family, too? Because I did. Luke was the one who sent me down the path to find them. And I took them all out…*for me.* For my vengeance." His voice thickened. "I enjoyed their deaths."

If that didn't make him *bad,* then…

"T-take off your gloves, okay? I don't want to be with the Reaper. I want to be with Cass. This time...just us, all right? Just us." Another tear.

He *hated* her tears.

Cass took off his gloves. He dropped them onto the nightstand, then he climbed onto the bed. He stretched out, and his hands curled around the bottom wooden slat on the headboard. It was an old-fashioned bed, nothing fancy. And the board he gripped? He could crush it. Actually, Cass feared he *would* crush it.

But Amber had moved to stand near him. Gazing into his eyes, she let her towel fall to the floor. "You fear touching."

He feared killing *her*.

"But I don't. So I get to touch you, all over. And you get to see...that I trust you. I trust you completely, Cass, and soon, I hope you'll trust me the same way."

Why? Why did she trust him? He'd just told her what a damn monster he was.

"You saved me today." She stared straight into his eyes and he had the eerie feeling that, for the first time, someone was truly seeing *him*.

Not the Reaper. The man.

Cass swallowed. "I knew I couldn't die." Or rather, that he couldn't stay dead.

"Other than my family, no one has ever risked so much for me. I saw the wounds on you. You were battered from head to toe. And...even back at the hotel, when Gregory came crashing in to our room, you protected me then, too. You covered me with your body, and the glass went into your back."

His gaze slid over her. "Didn't…want you hurt."

"I didn't think my knight in shining armor would be Death."

His gaze jerked back up to hers.

"I was wrong." She slid onto the bed. Onto *him.* She straddled him and her legs slid along either side of his hips. "I won't be wrong again. Not about you."

She didn't understand…

Amber bent and pressed a kiss to his lips. Not some chaste, soft kiss. Sexy as hell. Her tongue slid over his lips, then thrust into his mouth. She stroked him with her tongue, making his whole body shudder.

His cock was fully erect and because of the way she'd positioned herself on him, his length shoved against her sex. She was wet and soft, and he wanted to arch up and sink into her.

"Not yet," Amber whispered against his mouth. "Because I'm just getting started."

Then she began to kiss a path down his neck. She stopped to lick and suck the skin right over his racing pulse.

He growled.

She nipped him.

His eyes squeezed shut. *Fuck, yes.*

Then she was pressing her lips to his chest.

His hands tightened on the wood and he heard a low creak.

She licked his nipple. His hips arched against her.

"Ah…trying to get my attention? I was working my way down there but…" Then she eased her body back, moving the sweet heat of her sex away from his aching cock.

"No—" Cass began.

But then her mouth was on him. She curled her luscious lips around his cock and she sucked him in. His eyes nearly rolled back in his head and the wood splintered beneath his grip.

She sucked and she licked and she drove him insane.

But he didn't touch her.

Wouldn't.

Cass grabbed for the second slat of wood that made up the headboard. His fingers locked around it. "Amber…no more. I need *in* you."

Her head lifted. "I thought you *were* in my mouth."

His teeth ground together…

"Oh," she murmured, obviously not understanding just how dangerous it was to tease him. "You mean *in* me…this way?" And then she was straddling him once again. Her hand moved between them and she guided his cock to her core. He thrust up just as she arched her hips down against him.

Tight. Hot. Heaven.

He withdrew, then plunged deep. She was gasping and rocking against him. Going up and down, but it wasn't enough—

That second slat shattered.

He shoved upward, moving fast, and he saw the alarm in her eyes.

But Cass just tumbled her back onto the bed, trapping her beneath him. His hands fisted around the bedcovers, grabbing tight, and then he was shoving deep into her, controlling the thrusts and filling her completely.

She came for him, crying out her pleasure as her sex contracted around him. He let himself go even as the pulses of her release rocked around him. He emptied into her, lodged deep in her tight, hot sex, never, fucking *ever* wanting to leave her.

The pleasure was just as hot as before, just as consuming. It seemed to burn right through his body, pushing away the coldness that had surrounded him for so long. A cold that had gone soul-deep.

Until he found Amber.

I won't let her go. I can't. His head lifted.

She was smiling at him. "See?" Amber whispered. "I was right to trust you."

Don't be so sure, sweets. Because he wasn't the kind of man that anyone should trust.

***

Gregory knew when he was fucking in trouble. And when the Lord of the Dark yanked a guy from a plane…

Hello, trouble.

Luke Thorne had yanked him from that plane and taken him back down to earth. Now he was in the middle of freaking nowhere. Luke stood in front of him and he knew he had to tread damn carefully.

"Want to tell me why you were circling like a hawk?"

This was his moment. Gregory lifted his chin. "Because I'm the hunter you want, not Cass. I'm the one who can bring back your bounty. The Reaper has gone soft. You can't count on him any longer."

Luke's dark brows rose. "Oh, really?" He didn't sound convinced.

"He won't bring her to you. The woman you're after? Amber?" *Plant the doubt. Twist it inside of him.* "He's fucking her."

Luke's face changed. Went absolutely dark.

So much for the stories about Luke having a mate. The guy was obviously involved with Cass's bounty. Gregory could use that involvement. "He's going to try and keep her. He's—"

Luke had wrapped one claw-tipped hand around his throat. Using that grip, Luke lifted Gregory into the air. "You're lying to me."

Could Luke tell when a paranormal lied? The stories said maybe but…Gregory had taken precautions. He wasn't the first vampire to go up against Luke. "I didn't *see* them fucking with my own eyes, but I saw him. I saw how he looked at her. He wants her, bad, and he's not going to give her up to you. The guy has fallen under her spell—"

Luke tossed him away. "The fool wouldn't be the first."

"He's not going to bring her to you. He's going to run."

Luke's wings spread behind him. "That would be a mistake."

"I know you made a deal with him, but he's going to betray you. That's why you need me." He was totally playing in the big leagues now. Gregory took a quick breath and rose to his full height. Luke had literally yanked him off that plane. Gregory didn't even know where the damn thing was now. Crashed? Burning in a million pieces?

He was in the woods, facing off against Luke, and he knew he had to sell his story. Sell it *hard*. "Have you tried summoning him?" It was an obvious choice for Luke. He *should* have just summoned Cass and gotten his prey. Simple. But the very fact that Luke was standing in front of him—and there was no Reaper anywhere to be seen—meant that trouble was brewing. "Because my money says you have...but he's not jumping to follow your command, is he? He's too distracted by *her*."

"Why were you circling around the crash site?"

"Because I wanted the bounty." Gregory had found that a mix of truth and lies worked best in life. "And I knew he was going to pull some shit like this. I mean, he killed Ivan to cover his tracks."

Luke's eyes narrowed. "Ivan?"

"Yeah, yeah, you head back to Mississippi, and you'll find that poor bear shifter is nothing but a pile of ash." He'd made sure of that. "Cass killed Ivan, then he stole the plane from the guy's hangar. Cass—because he and I go way back, he thought I'd be on his side." Gregory gave a sad shake of his head. "But I know better than to go up against the Lord of the Dark." Was Luke buying his story? "Cass *told* me he was going to wreck the plane. He wanted you to think that the girl was dead. But really...he was just planning to take her away from you."

Luke stared straight into his eyes. And Gregory hoped like hell that the old magic he'd used would hold up.

Magic he'd gotten courtesy of other vampires. Some vampires who were still hoping to break the bond that Luke held over them.

You won't ever see this revolt coming.

"I bet he scared her," Gregory murmured, hoping to focus Luke's attention on the woman. "I mean, she wouldn't have known what he planned. Not until the plane started to go down. She would have been afraid, probably been screaming…"

Luke's wings flapped. "Where will he go?"

"Not to you, that's for damn sure. You can sit at your place in Key West forever, and Cass won't show."

"He *will,*" Luke fired back. "I have what he wants."

"You sure about that?" Gregory lifted his brows. "Like I told you, I saw the way he looked at *her.*"

The ground trembled beneath him.

Just like Leo…the woman matters to Luke, too.

She truly would be the perfect weapon. If Gregory could just fucking find her. "He's in Florida, we know that." Because Cass's plane had crashed in Florida. Gregory continued, speaking quickly, "I can get her back—"

"How do you plan to kill the unkillable?"

"We don't need to kill him." He had a better plan. "You…the stories say no one can get out of your prison. We just have to catch Cass, and then you can lock him up. Problem solved for *both* of us. He's gone, you get your prey back and I…"

"What do you get?"

You'll see. "I'll be the hunter you call for business. The deals you make in the future will all be with me."

Luke never so much as blinked. "How the fuck do you think you will find him now? The Reaper will move fast."

"I know him." Simple. True. "For years, he was family to me."

"Family can screw you over," Luke murmured.

"I'm the one who taught him to hunt. I'm the one who helped him make his first kill." Even after all of that, Cass had still betrayed him. *He hunted vampires. He picked the wrong side.* "I can think like him. I can predict his moves. Right now, he's hiding. He went to ground, probably in some shady motel where people don't ask questions."

Luke growled. *Right. You're angry, aren't you? Because Cass is in that shady motel with the mysterious Amber.*

"He'll wait for night, and then he'll go out."

"And I'll have nearly every paranormal in the state looking for him," Luke said flatly. "I have eyes everywhere, so I don't see why I could possibly need *you.*"

"Because Cass can and will kill any of those paranormals who get close to him. But he won't kill me." Gregory puffed out his chest. "Family, you know? I'm the only family he has left. That's why he hasn't killed me before and it's why he *won't* kill me now. So you put out word to all those under your power. You get them to look for the Reaper and his pretty new prize. But then…when you get a tip about him, if you're smart, you'll call me. You'll let me be the one to take him down because if he gets his hands on you…maybe you'll be the one who dies." It was a risk, saying those words. But everyone had always wondered…

Can the Reaper kill the Lord of the Dark?

Luke's jaw locked. "I don't really give a fuck what becomes of the Reaper. If you can get close to him, then you *can* get Amber away from him, correct?"

"Yes." Luke hadn't given him the answer he'd sought but…

"She's what matters to me. Get her back for me, and you and I—we *will* deal."

Interesting. "And the Reaper?"

Luke's eyes heated. "If he's touched her, then I'll throw him in my prison and he will *never* get out."

Fair enough. Smiling, Gregory held out his hand. "Deal?"

Luke's fingers curled around his. "Deal."

Satisfaction curled in his gut like a heavy snake. "You know..." Gregory murmured as his hand still gripped Luke's. "I know one witch in particular who lives in the area. Marguerite has been in Florida for years. And she can search from above for us."

Luke jerked his hand free of Gregory's.

"Why don't you use that dark power of yours?" Gregory pressed. "Call her in on the hunt...and let her know I'm on your side. She owes me, and Marguerite will come running to your aid so fast when she knows I'm here." He smiled at Luke.

Smiled...

And plotted the bastard's death.

CHAPTER TWELVE

"So…what's the deal with the scythe?" Amber's index finger traced over the tattoo on Cass's back. "Another gift from Luke?"

"Yes."

Isn't he the generous one? Only, Luke wasn't. Not under normal circumstances. "Why did he give it to you?"

"Sometimes, it's hard to get touching-close to my prey. When I can't get physically close enough to my target, I can throw the scythe. It *always* finds its prey."

So Luke had given him the magical scythe so that Cass would be even better at killing. "Always?" *It never misses?*

"Yes."

Swallowing, she pulled away from him. A quick glance outside showed her that night had fallen. She knew that meant they'd be leaving soon. Running again. Amber rose from the bed and dressed. Her clothes were relatively blood free but Cass…

He rose, too, and he stared down at his body. "Think anyone will notice that my clothes are soaked in blood while I'm walking around town?"

She bit her lip, then waved her hand.

Instantly, fresh clothes appeared on his body.

Cass stiffened.

Well, hell, since he gets new clothes...She waved her hand and fresh clothes replaced her rather grimy garments.

"How'd you do that?" His voice rasped at her.

She offered him a wan smile. "Magic." She'd been hauling that suitcase around before not because she needed the change of clothes—she'd been hiding the Blade of Truth in with the other garments. She'd lied when she gave him the story about the bag containing everything she owned. The bag *had* contained the thing of most value to her—the knife.

Suddenly, he was right in front of her. "You never told me...what you are."

No, she hadn't.

"Trust cuts both ways, you know."

She supposed it did. "My mother was a fairy."

Her father...he'd been something entirely different.

Shock filled his gaze. "Fairies haven't been around for hundreds of years."

Amber shrugged. "So I look good for my age." Her head tipped back as she stared up at him.

"All of the fairies are dead."

"All of the *full* blooded fairies are dead," Amber corrected. "I'm still here. I just don't have as much magic as I used to possess." Due to the whole missing wings bit. "Once upon a time…" Wasn't that how the best stories began? Or the worst ones? "Fairies had the purest magic in the world. They were supposedly the first of the 'good' paranormals. Always wanting to help people, always wanting to fix things." To tinker with the world. She swallowed. "But then others found out that their magic could be taken, that it could be tapped if you cut the wings off a fairy. But what our enemies didn't get—or maybe, maybe they just didn't care—was that without our wings, the fairies died."

He'd put his gloves back on. Her gaze lingered on those gloves as a lump rose in her throat.

Someone had cut off his hands…just as someone had cut off her wings.

Only… "I think those gloves are made of fairy wings."

He stepped back. She stopped her lips from trembling and stared him in the eyes. "I knew it, the first time you touched my scars with them. It was like…a hum of power hit me."

His gaze turned horrified.

"Fairy wings or angel wings...even before you touched me, I knew it had to be one or the other. Nothing else could harness power that way."

He started to rip off the gloves.

"Stop." Her heart hurt.

He'd gone pale. "How can you bear for me to touch you?"

"Some fairies...they gave up power from their wings willingly. To help others. Maybe...maybe that's where your magic came from. Maybe a fairy wanted to help so she or he gave the magic that allows you to touch." That was what she had to tell herself. "Without the gloves, you will kill everyone you touch."

"But when you look at the gloves..."

She remembered what she'd lost.

"How did you survive without them?" His voice was gruff.

Forcing a smile, she said, "I told you...my mother was a fairy. My father was something quite different."

He stared at her. Waiting.

"A demon." Her confession came out as a whisper because it was her shame. "My mother was a fairy, but my father was the darkest of the dark. A demon. The baddest of the paranormals. My mother shouldn't have loved him, it was forbidden. But she did. Light and dark blending together…"

"He said you were light and dark." Cass raked a hand through his hair. "Luke said…he *knew.* All along, he's known what you were."

"Luke has always known."

His hand fell back to his side. "What is he to you? Enemy? Former lover? *What?*"

"He's someone who scares me. Someone I *don't* want to ever face again." And this was the moment of truth. "I told you my secrets."

"Not all, not about Luke—"

"Tell me yours. What did he offer you? What did Luke promise you if you brought me back? How much did he pay you?"

His brilliant blue eyes glittered.

"Cass?"

"A mate."

This time, she was the one who took a step back.

He lifted his hands and glared down at the gloves. "Someone I could touch with my own hands. Someone who wanted me and wasn't repelled by the Reaper. That is what Luke promised—*she* is what Luke promised me, if I just brought you to him."

Her hand lifted and pressed to her chest. For some reason, her chest was burning. "And you're going to let her go? This…this perfect mate out there? Because if you betray Luke, if you don't take me to him, you *will* lose her. I know Luke. He'll make sure that you never find her."

He just stared back at her.

They'd just made love—no, maybe they'd just fucked—and now she was feeling completely blindsided. She'd believed him when he said Luke wouldn't get her again. But now… "Were you lying to me?"

"Amber…"

She couldn't run away from him. Not yet. Forty-eight hours hadn't passed. *OhmyGod.* Had she really only been with him for such a short time? Because it was hard for her to see past him. He seemed to have filled her life.

Think, think! "Luke will be looking for us."

"No." Cass shook his head. "He will wait for me to deliver you to his island. He isn't going to be searching for us."

Yes, he will. Because I called out to him.

"He *will* be looking." She exhaled and tried to think. To plan. "So he'll probably spread the word to every paranormal he can find…telling them what you look like. What I look like. And they'll report back to him as soon as they spot us."

"You know him well."

Too well.

"If all he had to do was tell the other paranormals to look for you…" A furrow appeared between his brows. "Then why didn't he do that sooner? Why did he wait and have me look for you?"

"I don't know why he's suddenly so hot to find me." To her, that just meant big old danger in big, bright letters. "But I *do* know why he didn't turn to the other paranormals sooner. I'm…I guess you could say I'm Luke's dirty little secret."

Fury flashed on his face.

"Things have changed, though. I—" *Dammit, tell him.* "When the plane was going down, I called out to Luke. I was afraid and I screamed for him in my mind."

If possible, his face hardened even more. "You and Luke must have one damn strong connection for you to be able to do that." Jealousy boiled beneath his words.

She couldn't look him in the eye. "We do. And because of that…because he probably thinks I'm hurt, he's going to do everything in his power to find me. The secret will be out. He'll use anyone and everyone to hunt me."

His eyes were slits of blue fury. "Why don't you just send him another psychic message? With that *bond* you two share? Let him know you're alive and well."

"Because if I do that, he'll lock on me. Luke's always been stronger than I am. If I give him the chance, he'll grab hold of our link and take control of it. He'll find me. He'll find you." And that *wouldn't* end well. Briskly, she nodded. "We should go. Stick to the backroads and put as much distance between us and him as possible." Because she knew Luke was close by…but she didn't tell Cass that part. She'd already overshared enough. "If you…still plan on not turning me over, that is. If you plan—"

He grabbed her wrists. Held tight. "Fuck the mate I *don't* have."

What?

"You think I could go to another after being with you?" Then he was kissing her—so hard and wild. As if she were the only woman in the world. As if she mattered to him.

Maybe she did. Maybe…

"I don't know her. I know you. I want *you.* I told you…Luke will not hurt you. No one will ever hurt you. Not while I'm near. I'm breaking the deal with him, and I don't care what it costs me."

Hope rose within her, almost painful to feel.

"I chose you, Amber. Luke can fuck off. I'm not afraid of him. Never have been."

She threw her arms around him and held tight.

His arms closed around her. "You don't…fear me, do you?"

She buried her face against his chest. "No, I don't." Though she did fear what would happen when Luke learned of his betrayal. "Maybe we can run far enough…maybe he'll never find us." She looked up at him.

But…Cass shook his head.

He shook his head.

She pushed against his chest and backed away. 'You…don't want to leave with me?"

"I want to be with you, hell, yes, but I'm not the kind of man who will spend his life running. I won't always look over my shoulder, waiting for Luke to appear or trying to dodge every paranormal creature on earth because I'm worried someone will report me to Luke. He will *not* always threaten you."

He didn't get it—

"I'll make a new deal with him. I'll get him to back off you. You'll be safe."

No. Didn't he get it? "Luke won't take a new deal. You go to Luke without me, and you'll just piss him off. He'll toss you in a cell and you won't see daylight again."

"You underestimate me." He lifted a hand. "If I have to do it, I will kill the bastard."

"*No!*" The sharp cry burst from her.

And she knew she'd just given too much away.

"You…care about him." The jealousy was back, grating in his voice.

Dammit, dammit, dammit! "I don't want him dead, okay? I'm not looking to kill anyone. That's not who I am." Amber marched for the door.

"Look, let's just get out of here while we can. This place is way too close to the crash site. We need some more distance, and the night won't last forever."

She yanked open the door. Amber heard his footsteps behind her. She stepped into the night.

His gloved hand curled around her shoulder. "Do you love him?"

Her eyes closed. "It's not like you think, okay?" She glanced back at him. "Haven't you heard? The big, bad Lord of the Dark *has* a mate. He's obsessed with the lovely Mina, not with me."

"Do you love him?" Cass repeated.

Her heart ached. "We need to go."

His jaw clenched. "You do."

"There are—I can't—" Her breath heaved out. "There are things I *can't* tell you. You're better off not knowing, okay? Can't you just trust me? There is *nothing* sexual between us. I'm not pining away for him. He's not pining for me."

His gaze searched hers. "What kind of man would you love?"

The question actually gave her pause. "Someone who would fight the dark for me." Her smile felt sad. "And the light." Because that was what it would truly take.

His hand fell away.

Right. She wanted the impossible.

They hurried into the night. The old pickup was still there, waiting for them, but Cass steered her around it.

"In case the guy called the cops, we don't want that thing on the road." He pointed to an older sedan. "That one won't be equipped with any GPS tracker or alarms. Want to work your magic and get it going for us?"

Sure. She headed toward the car. Cass opened the driver side door for her—mostly because the guy used some super strength and yanked that locked door right open. She was pretty sure he'd smashed the lock to hell and back. She slid under the front seat, dipping beneath the dash and—

"Someone is looking for you." The voice was low, feminine, and coming from the dark.

Amber's head snapped up, rapping into the dash.

"You have me confused with someone else," Cass said flatly.

"I don't think so. It's hard to mistake the Reaper. I've never forgotten you."

Amber slid out of the car and she found herself at Cass's side. A woman stood about ten feet away, a woman clad in shadows and darkness. Her long, thick hair was midnight black, and it trailed over her shoulders. She lifted her hand and pointed at Cass…and then at

Amber. "Everyone is searching. And I found you first. Luke will be very, very pleased with me."

Oh, crap. "Lady, you're confused. You're—"

The woman's lips parted as she laughed. Only that laugh sounded exactly like the call of a crow.

"Hell." Cass lunged forward and Amber saw the flash of his scythe. He'd pulled his weapon and he was going to use it on that woman.

"No!" Amber grabbed for his arm.

But it was too late. He'd sliced out with the scythe, only…

The woman vanished. She seemed to turn into thick, dark fog and then—a dozen crows appeared where she'd been. Those crows were all calling out, still using that taunting cry that had been her laugh, and they flew up into the air, moving together and swirling high above Amber and Cass.

Amber blinked as she stared after them. "We have a problem."

"A big fucking one." The scythe vanished. "Get that sweet ass in the car. Because this time, *I'm* the one who's being hunted."

And the crows—that woman—Amber knew she'd be running right to Luke.

CHAPTER THIRTEEN

Cass slammed his foot down on that gas pedal, knowing that time was running out. The woman who'd been in that parking lot—she'd been a very, very powerful witch. And every single crow—Cass had counted twelve of those bastards—would have gone to spread the word about his location.

"Luke isn't giving me the time I was promised." His hands tightened around the wheel. *Because the guy knows I'm breaking our deal?* How would Luke know that?

"We can get away," Amber said but her voice sounded uncertain.

They'd already driven for an hour, blazing down the dark, deserted road.

"We just have to keep going," she continued but she shivered next to him, as if suddenly cold. "We can't stop. We—"

The sedan rounded the curve and the headlights fell on the two men in the road. Two men...and the two wolves who were at their sides.

Cass didn't even slow down. He shoved his foot down harder on the accelerator. "*Hold on.*"

"Cass…"

But the wolves were charging at him. They leapt onto the hood of the car and then the beasts came crashing right through the windshield. Glass shattered around them, and the big, white wolf sank its teeth into Cass's arm.

The car careened to the right, spinning, and it slammed into a tree.

Cass drove his fist at the wolf, again and again, and the beast wouldn't let him go. He could hear footsteps closing in…

"Cass?" Fear roughened Amber's voice.

He glanced at her. She hadn't been hurt in the accident, but the other wolf's fangs were now inches from her face.

Screw this. He brought his left hand to his mouth and used his teeth to yank off the glove. He brought that hand toward the wolf—

The beast that had been attacking him backed away, howling.

And the wolf that had been *far* too close to Amber retreated.

Cass took off his other glove. "They're surrounding us." He eased out a slow breath. "When we get out of the car, just stay behind me." He would take them out. Amber would be safe.

"You're…going to kill them all?"

Grimly, he told her, "I'll do what's necessary." He shoved open his door, knocking broken glass out of his way.

Amber scrambled out behind him—but she didn't *stay* behind him. Instead, she put herself right at his side. "There are a lot of them..."

Two fully shifted werewolves. The two men he'd seen before—he wasn't sure *what* those guys were yet. But they'd pulled out guns and aimed them at him. A crow called from overhead.

Figured. The witch had joined the party.

"Not so many. Only four," Cass said, smiling. The witch didn't count since she was still in crow form. "This will barely take any effort."

"Don't be too sure..."

The taunt came from the right.

Cass's head turned and he found himself staring into Gregory's gleaming eyes.

"Got you," Gregory said. The crow flew down and landed on his shoulder. He reached up and stroked the crow's head. "Do you remember Marguerite? She was Hycim's lover...and she was *quite* pissed when you killed her man."

"Hycim?" Amber whispered. She inched closer to Cass.

Cass swept his gaze toward the crow. "Didn't ask about his lovers...didn't care. He was a dead man walking."

More crows called from overhead.

"The men here...they all followed Hycim." Gregory stalked a bit closer. "Werewolves *and* vampires."

The two men with guns bared their fangs.

Since when did vamps need guns to attack?

Since they're trying to take me out.

"We gave you a home, Reaper. We *helped* you," Gregory continued in a voice thick with fury. "Then you turned on us."

"The vamps I took out were rabid. They were killing everything in their path and I—"

"You were the good foot soldier for Luke. Doing *exactly* what he said." Disgust dripped from every word. "Well...here's your chance to redeem yourself. Because I am going to give you *one* chance. Only one."

Cass kept his body loose.

"Do you know what Luke wants to do to you?" Gregory asked. Another crow swooped down and landed near the white wolf. "He's going to lock you up. He thinks you tried to escape with Amber here...that you wanted to keep her for yourself."

I do.

"So he's going to throw you into the prison on his island. You will *never* see daylight again."

"That can't happen," Amber whispered.

It won't.

"Then he's going to take her..." Gregory pointed to Amber. "And he's going to do whatever the hell it is that he wants with her. You won't be able to stop him. You'll be long gone. Wasting away in that cell."

Cass swept his gaze around the group, already planning just who he would kill first. Gregory was obviously the most dangerous. *Should have taken him out long ago.* But the white wolf was closest…

"That's option one," Gregory explained. "But there is another way for all of this to end."

"Can't wait to hear it," Cass called. *Like I give a shit.*

"Option two…you touch that sweet piece of ass right next to you."

Cass narrowed his eyes on Gregory.

"You put your hand on Amber, and you kill her. She's the person Luke wants so badly…so that means she's the person who will hurt him the most. Kill her and strike back at Luke. His days of ruling are over. It's time for a new power."

Cass shook his head. "Here I thought you wanted to be Luke's right hand man. That was just bullshit wasn't it? You want to get close to him because…you're just like Hycim." And being close to Luke, getting Luke's trust…*you think that will make him easier to kill, don't you, Gregory?*

Gregory smiled. "Who do you think gave Hycim his fucking ideas?" Then he laughed. "You killed the wrong guy so long ago. I was the one who *made* Hycim. He was just a wolf before I found him. I made him stronger. Just as I will make *all* of my followers stronger. I've been on this earth for thousands of years. I know all the magic out there. I've *used* the magic out there, and I'll use it again. Again and again and again until I have everything that I desire."

"You…" Amber's voice rose. "You told Hycim to take the fairy wings, didn't you?"

"Fairy wings?" Then he laughed once more. "Ah, yes, I'd almost forgotten that. He'd found the last fairy on earth. He wanted her wings and I told him to cut them off her. Fairy wings always held so much power."

Cass saw Amber tremble near him.

"But after Hycim's death," Gregory rolled back his shoulders, "I lost those wings. Couldn't find them fucking anywhere."

And Cass had wiped out the guy's would-be army when Luke sent him after Hycim's men. "You were left with jackshit."

"I had to start all over again!" Gregory's voice boomed out. "But I was patient. I waited…and now I have Luke right where I want him. He trusts me. *His* mistake. I will get killing-close and he won't know it until it's too late."

"You can't kill Luke," Amber yelled.

"I can't…" Gregory nodded. "But Cass can."

Maybe.

"You can kill anyone…and with the right motivation, I know that you will." Gregory inclined his head toward Cass. "I didn't really think you'd go for option two. I'd hoped so…it would have made my life easier, but you've always been a difficult sonofabitch, you know?"

The scythe appeared in Cass's hand. *Gregory will die first.*

"And there's that…" Gregory glared at the scythe. "Luke plays favorites, doesn't he? Giving you that lovely weapon…and, of course, your gloves."

"I'm not wearing them right now." Cass sent him a cold smile. "All the better to kill you."

A crow called out behind Cass. He stiffened. That call…had it come from *inside* the car?

"No," Gregory told him flatly. "All the better for me to distract you."

Cass spun around.

Not just one crow was in the car. *Two.* And each crow had a glove clenched tightly in its beak.

He lunged for the birds, but they flew away.

"Tell me this isn't as bad as I think it is," Amber muttered.

Cass spun back to face Gregory. Right at the vamp's side, the crows—a dozen of them—rushed together and reformed—Marguerite. She had the gloves on her hands.

Cass threw his scythe. It tumbled end over end and—

Marguerite burst into twelve crows once more. The scythe hit one crow but missed the others. *Shit. It still hit the prey…but it didn't stop her.*

"I always thought you didn't need the gloves. I mean, your whole purpose is to kill. So why *not* kill?" Gregory demanded. "Marguerite, love, take those gloves far the fuck away."

No!

But the remaining crows were already flying high into the sky, and the two werewolves were closing in. Once more, Cass summoned his scythe.

"Got the gloves," Gregory murmured, as if checking off items on his list. "And now I'll be taking that bounty. Amber…I do have plans for you."

The two werewolves leapt at Cass. His scythe cut into one, sending a spray of blood and making the beast howl in pain.

Cass's hand flew out and touched the second wolf. It dropped to the ground, dead.

Bullets blasted into him, hitting his chest, his shoulder. He reached for Amber, wanting to shield her.

No! Can't touch her!

He caught himself just before his fingers would have touched her shoulder.

She stared at him, her eyes wide and horrified. *I'll keep you safe. I swear.* Then Cass was rushing toward the men with guns. They kept firing. The bullets hit him again—one in his knee, making his right leg give way. But he was close enough…

He touched the shooter even as he went down.

The bastard died still gripping his gun.

The second shooter was firing at Amber. When Cass had run at the vampires with guns, she'd had to follow him. *Fucking magical link. I'm so sorry, sweets.* He had to protect her.

Cass yanked the weapon from the dead man and gave a loud whistle.

The second shooter glanced at him. "Enjoy hell," Cass said. He fired. His bullet blasted straight into the vamp's heart. The guy stumbled back…

That won't kill a vamp. I need more. I need—

The injured vamp smiled, baring his fangs, and then he turned his gun toward Cass. He fired—

My heart. Cass felt the bullet sink into him.

"No!" Amber screamed.

Darkness was closing around him. It was a darkness that wouldn't last. It never did…but…

Amber.

He saw her. The vamp was laughing and aiming his gun at her.

With the last of his strength, Cass summoned his scythe once more. Heaving up, he threw the weapon and it spun, a dizzying blur that ended—

When the vamp's head hit the ground.

Amber fell to her knees at Cass's side and her hands went to his chest. "Cass? Tell me that you're not dying."

"Won't...stay dead..." Talking was too hard. He could barely see her. "Only lasts...few minutes..."

She was trying to stop the blood flow. She was *wasting* precious time on him.

"G-get away...R-run..." Cass tried to tell her. Because he'd taken out four of those bastards...

A crow called out.

But he'd missed the witch.

And Gregory had vanished as soon as the bullets started flying.

"I won't leave you," Amber said. She was still touching him. Still holding him tight.

And he realized...she *couldn't* leave him. The fucking magical tie was still between them. She'd been trapped, been kept at his side all along. But now...

Now he was fading and she'd be vulnerable.

He'd made her vulnerable.

"D-deal..." He tried to call out. The word came only as a whisper.

He wanted to deal. He wanted to trade. He wanted to do *anything* to keep Amber.

But his eyes closed. His heart stopped. And he saw hell once more.

***

The crows were cawing all around her. She *hated* that sound.

"Quite strange to see him die, isn't it?" Gregory said. He was back. Appearing from the dark, closing in on her.

Cass was still on the ground. His scythe had vanished. *But the gun is still here.* She grabbed the gun from Cass's hand and spun around, aiming it right at Gregory.

He froze, then he laughed. "Come on, love. I'm ancient. Those bullets won't do much damage to me at all."

The crows flew behind him. She caught a glimpse of Cass's gloves. The crows were in a frenzy.

"Let me guess…he used those magical cuffs on you, right? I mean, why else would you be at his side?"

Why else indeed? Maybe because there was no way she'd leave him alone. Maybe because at his side—that was just where she wanted to be.

"It will take a few moments for him to rise." Gregory took another step toward her. "By the time he does, you'll be dead."

"Or you will be."

Gregory laughed. "You are fun."

"And *you* are crazy. You think you can go up against Luke? You think he doesn't see your betrayal coming?" If she kept talking, maybe she could buy enough time for Cass to rise. "He does...Luke *knows* what you're planning."

Gregory wasn't laughing any longer.

"If you were dumb enough to meet him face-to-face, then he would have read your betrayal right in your eyes."

"Bullshit." But she thought she detected a note of fear in his voice.

"He knows..."

"The only thing he *knows* is that Cass was fucking you. That bit of news sure pissed off Luke." Gregory took another step toward her. The crows circled him. "It made him want your lover's head on a stick. Or rather...his sorry ass tossed in a cell. So Luke made a deal with me. I take out Cass...I get close enough to put him out of commission, and then I get whatever I want."

"I hate to break it to you, but Luke lied." She shrugged. "It's what he does." One of her hands was still on Cass's chest, waiting for his heart to beat again.

It has to beat. He has to come back to me.

Her other hand was curled around the gun.

"If you're smart, you'll get the hell out of here," she warned. "You'll run fast and you'll hope that Luke never finds you. Because if he does, he'll make you wish for death."

"Haven't you heard? Luke doesn't get his hands dirty. He hires out that work to fools like Cass there." And Gregory advanced another step.

"Don't," Amber bit off.

"But I must. You see, I really do have this all planned. I'm going to kill *you,* and then I'm going to let Luke and Cass fight it out over your dead body. After all, Luke will be arriving any moment. He's been so desperate to get you back."

The crows called out again.

"So you have to be dead *before* Luke arrives. You'll be dead, literally at Cass's feet. When he wakes up and finds you that way, I'm counting on him going crazy. And the man who'll be in that crazy path?" He nodded once, obviously pleased with his plan. "Luke. Cass will go for him, and the Lord of the Dark will die."

"No." She kept her gaze on him. There was a serious flaw with his logic. "Cass will know *you* are the one who hurt me. Not Luke. You're the one he'll come for."

His voice dropped to a whisper as he told her, "I won't be here. It will just be Cass, your dead body...and Luke. And here's the thing, dear Amber...I think Cass gave you his heart. I think he's finally—after centuries of having *nothing*—found a woman that he let get close."

Her hand was over his heart right then. *And it's still not beating.*

"Cass won't have a sane thought when he wakes and you're dead. He'll know only rage. And even if he *did* try to fight through that fury...Luke will be blaming him. Luke will see *him* as your killer. So Luke will attack. They'll fight, and I'm sure it will be epic."

She couldn't let that happen. She *wouldn't* let that happen.

Why wasn't Cass waking up?

"So...this little chat has been fun—always nice to have my brilliance appreciated—but it's time for you to die." He snapped his fingers together. "Marguerite, love, why don't you go for her eyes?"

Distracting. That was what he was doing. His witch was coming for her eyes and Amber knew Gregory would attack her at the same moment.

Amber aimed and fired—again and again and again. She shot at the crows as they flew at her and they dropped to the ground. *One, two, three, four–*

Cass's heart jerked beneath her hand. *He was coming back!* She just had to hold off the attack a little longer.

Bam! Bam!

*Five, six crows down...*Did she have to kill them all before Marguerite stopped the attack? Amber fired again—

And at that last shot, all of the crows just fell from the sky. They hit the ground and took the form of Marguerite. A very still Marguerite.

"Out of bullets?" Gregory was right in front of her.

"Not yet." She fired at him.

The bullet blasted right into his chest but…

He was a vampire. That wouldn't kill him.

She tried to fire again. But the gun just clicked.

Now I'm out.

The fear must have flashed on her face because he laughed again. Gregory grabbed her and yanked her up. His hands locked around her neck. "Can't have too many wounds on you. Has to look as if his touch alone killed you…"

She slammed her forehead against his. He swore and his hands tightened on her neck.

He didn't let her go. Without her wings, she was no match for him. Barely stronger than a human. And she called out desperately for help…using the last of her strength to send that psychic call…knowing there was one thing she had to do…

Luke…don't hurt Cass! Don't!

She opened the psychic path between them, pulling Luke in once more as she fought to send out that message—

Snap.

She was staring straight into Gregory's eyes when he broke her neck. He smiled at her and then he dropped her to the ground.

***

Gregory rubbed his hands together. Amber was at his feet, her body half-sprawled across Cass. Perfect positioning.

Humming, he turned and headed toward Marguerite. Her eyes were wide open and staring at nothing. The gloves were still on her hands.

"Don't mind if I do," he murmured as he took those gloves and slid them onto his own hands. What a perfect fit.

Overhead, lightning flashed across the sky and thunder rumbled. Luke would be coming soon…after all, Gregory had called him while his werewolves had been attacking Cass and Amber. The bullets had started flying and he'd known it was the perfect moment to bring in the Lord of the Dark.

Now it was time to retreat and watch the fireworks. He was sure the battle would be something to see…the stuff of legends.

He'd always wanted to be legendary.

CHAPTER FOURTEEN

Cass's eyes flew open and he sucked in a deep gulp of air. "*Amber!*"

His hands shot out as he sat up and…

And Amber was on him. His hands had curled around her shoulders. His *bare* hands.

He let her go instantly, but she just sagged back onto him. Her body was limp. Lifeless.

No, *no*. He slid from beneath her, terrified of again touching her with his bare hands. Her eyes were closed, her body slack on the ground. "*Amber?*" He pressed his mouth to hers, trying to breathe for her as he'd done before.

Don't do this. Please, fucking please…stay with me.

Thunder boomed overhead. Lightning flashed in the sky.

And he couldn't look away from her.

"Please come back!" He was begging and he didn't care. This was *Amber*. His gaze flew over her. Her hands were covered with blood—his blood. He remembered her touching him.

Remembered the fear on her face. He'd wanted her to run because Gregory was still out there...

But she couldn't run. I tied her to me and the forty-eight hours hasn't quite ended. Not yet...

His head shot up and he glanced around. Bodies littered the ground—the werewolves, the vampires and...Marguerite.

Where in the hell was Gregory?

Cass put his mouth against Amber's once more and tried to breathe for her. Her body...she looked perfect to him. He didn't see any wounds on her.

Did I do this? When I grabbed for her, did I kill her? Because his touch never left so much as a mark on his prey.

Horror iced his heart.

Amber isn't prey. Amber is everything.

Had he killed her? That first touch?

Or did Gregory hurt her while I couldn't stop him?

Because Cass had failed to protect her. *I should have fucking killed Gregory at the hotel.*

The ground shook. Lightning flashed, hitting a tree, and the air seemed to burn with the scent of ozone.

"Get away from her!"

Cass was crouched over Amber's body. His hands were on either side of her. His mouth just above hers.

"Reaper…" That snarling voice belonged to Luke. Cass knew it without looking up. So he didn't glance away from Amber.

More thunder rumbled. "Get your ass away from my sister," Luke roared.

Away from his—

Sister?

Cass's head whipped toward Luke. The Lord of the Dark's wings were fully extended, the scales gleaming.

My mother was a fairy, but my father was the darkest of the dark…a demon. Amber's words replayed in his head.

"I told you," Luke gritted out. "I wanted her back alive. *Alive.*"

Lightning flashed down on the ground just inches from Cass's right hand.

"She's not dead," Cass said because she *couldn't* be. *Don't be dead, Amber. Don't—*

Because he needed her. He…

Loved her?

His chest burned as the fear spread within him. *Did my touch do this?*

Lightning flashed again—only this time the lightning slammed into Cass's body. He jerked, his head whipping back as the pain blasted him, and then he found himself flying through the air and crashing into the side of the wrecked sedan.

Cass shook himself off and leapt to his feet. He ran at Luke—

But Luke was touching Amber's face, his hand tender on her cheek. "I can bring you back."

He could...Cass staggered to a stop. "Do it." His words were ragged. "*Help her.*"

Luke lifted Amber into his arms. He held her so carefully and when he looked down at her, there was grief on his face.

Sister.

Cass couldn't wrap his mind around that shit. Amber was the sister to the freaking ruler of the dark paranormals? No wonder she hadn't said anything about that particular connection.

Luke has too many enemies...if the truth got out, they'd use her.

They'd hurt her.

Just as she'd been hurt before.

But if she was Luke's sister...

Oh, hell, she's tied to Leo, too.

Cass swallowed the lump in his throat. "I..." *I need her. I have to get her back. Please, fucking...bring her back!*

Luke's wings flapped. His eyes glowed with power—a bright light that seemed to consume him and Amber. The light pulsed. It grew. It...

"She's not waking up." Cass rushed toward them.

Thunder rumbled again.

"Bring her back!" He wasn't pleading any longer. He was bellowing. The bastard had just said—

Luke's head turned to the right. He stared into the darkness. "I know you're there."

Cass summoned his scythe. Luke still held Amber, but she wasn't breathing. She wasn't moving at all. Her gorgeous eyes were closed and her body was too still. He put his blade right against Luke's throat. "Bring. Her. Back."

Luke's head turned toward Cass once more. The scythe cut him and blood trickled down Luke's throat. "You think you're going to kill me?"

"If you don't bring her back…"

"You believe I'm not fucking trying?" Luke's voice blasted. The ring on his finger glowed as brightly as his eyes. "She's not—"

"She's not yours," Leo said. The guy had just flown from the sky and landed right at Luke's side. "She never was…despite what you tried to do to her." He stared at Amber and grief sagged his shoulders. "She wasn't yours. She wasn't mine. And now she's…gone."

The hell she was. *"Get her back."* It was all he could manage. The world around him was going dark. Fury was welling inside of him. Fury and fear and pain. He'd just found Amber.

She wasn't supposed to be dead. She'd wanted them to run away, to start over together.

"Get her back," Cass shouted. "Or you both die." His scythe was still at Luke's throat. He would slice Luke, and then he would attack Leo.

They thought they were unstoppable. They thought they could play with the lives of everyone else. They were wrong. "She lives…or you both die." Because he wasn't some *lesser* paranormal who had to bow to them.

"You can't kill us," Leo snapped. "That's not the end fate has for us. You aren't *our* end—"

"Fuck fate," Cass snarled. "*She* is the only fate I care about. Amber. I want her back. You will bring her back. Do it—*now*." Because he couldn't stand the thought of her growing cold right there.

Amber is warmth. She's light. She's life.

My life.

"Bring her back…" Leo gave a bitter laugh. "So…what? So you can kill her with your touch again? *You* did this, Reaper. You're only made for death. You should have never been near her. You should have *never* hoped to have Amber as your own. She's so much better than you can ever dream. You didn't deserve her, you didn't—"

"Stop." Luke's voice. Flat. Cold.

The scythe had cut deeper into him.

But Luke stared at Cass with no fear in his glowing gaze. No, not fear.

Pity.

"Cass didn't kill her," Luke said.

Cass didn't kill her. He sucked in a deep breath.

"That bastard Gregory did. Amber told me…I *saw* through her eyes. He wanted me to think Cass had taken Amber's life. Wanted me to fly in with a fury and attack the Reaper." Luke's hold tightened on Amber's body. "He wants a battle. He wants me dead. He wants the Reaper out of the way. He wants chaos…"

Leo's body had stiffened. His gaze searched the darkness.

"I saw through her eyes," Luke said again. "I saw him smiling as he broke her neck."

Something in Cass seemed to break right then.

His gaze dipped to Amber's neck. "Bring her back." His voice had gone hoarse.

"I tried," Luke rasped. "But Amber is light and dark, a mix of our parents. I can only reach the dark…"

Cass yanked the scythe away from Luke's neck and shoved it against Leo's throat. "You're supposed to be the fucking good one."

Blood slid down Leo's throat.

"You pour your power into her, do you hear me? You give her your power and Luke gives her his…and you bring her back. You reach the light side of her, he pulls in the dark, and you *bring her back*." The breath he took burned Cass's lungs. "Give her your power or I will take your life right now."

Leo smiled at him. "Do you think you have to threaten me?" He moved closer to Amber and Luke, not seeming to even feel the wound at his throat as the scythe cut deeper into him. "I have loved her since the day she was born." Then Leo put his hand on her cheek. "She used to follow me around…always laughing. She *loved* me." Power swirled around him—the same brightness that had consumed Luke moments before.

"She loved me," Luke said, his voice still low. His eyes glowed. Lightning flashed once more. "Loved me so much that she gave up her wings to save me. She wasn't supposed to do that. She was *never* supposed to suffer for me."

Their light pulsed around her. Then it seemed to sink right *into* her.

But her eyes didn't open. She didn't breathe.

And the madness clawing at Cass's soul grew worse. "She's not waking!"

Lines of strain appeared on Leo's face. "Sleeping Beauty doesn't always wake…"

She wasn't fucking Sleeping Beauty. She was Amber. She was the woman the Reaper loved. And Death wasn't going to let her go.

Not ever.

"Heaven or hell," he growled. "Tell me where she is." And he put the scythe to his own throat. "Because I will go and bring her back. I will—"

Her lips parted. Amber sucked in a quick breath.

The light around her vanished. Her eyes opened—and they glowed with power.

"Amber!" Relief swept through him and he reached out for her. So desperate to hold her and feel her in his arms and—

Leo blasted him with a surge of white-hot power. Cass fell back, but lunged up—

Leo was in his path. "You want to kill her again? Because I don't know how many times we can bring her back."

*My touch…*In horror, Cass glanced at his bare hands.

Luke put Amber on her feet, and his hand stayed on her arm. He was touching her so carefully.

But Amber wasn't looking at him. She was staring at Cass, and her eyes were wide. "Cass?" She smiled at him. "You're okay! You didn't—you and Luke didn't—"

"We didn't kill each other," Luke said flatly. "Because I'm not a fucking idiot and I knew Gregory wanted us dead."

Gregory.

"Now that you're back in the land of the living…" Luke muttered, "It's time to finish some business." He put his hands on his hips and turned toward the line of trees to the right. "*Come out, come out…you soon to be headless vamp.*"

Amber was still staring at Cass.

"I believe you broke a deal with me, Gregory" Luke yelled. "And that is a very, very bad move. The kind of move that gets a vampire killed."

Gregory had broken Amber's neck.

Cass walked toward her.

Once more, Leo stepped in his path.

"Get the hell back," Cass snapped. "I won't hurt her."

"Like I'm supposed to believe the Reaper?"

But then Amber was the one shoving Leo out of her way. She threw her arms around Cass and held him tight.

His hands didn't touch her. His eyes squeezed shut.

She's warm. She's alive.

"Your heart wasn't beating," she said, her voice thick. "That scared the hell out of me." She looked up at him and there were tears on her lashes.

"You were dead," he told her. "And that scared the hell out of me."

Her gaze held his.

Gregory broke her neck.

Carefully, Cass bent his head. He pressed a tender kiss to her throat. "He will pay."

"Cass?" Fear hitched in his name.

He kissed her throat once again. "I'm sorry I didn't protect you." His wrist began to burn.

She gave a little gasp and he knew she felt that burn, too.

Their cuffs appeared, one on her wrist. One on his.

"The forty-eight hours are up," Cass told her, swallowing. "You're free." He pressed a kiss to her mouth. "And I swear, I will make sure that Gregory *never* hurts you again." He backed away from her. Then he reached for the cuff that surrounded his wrist. He shattered that cuff, breaking the bond between them.

Lightning was still flashing in the sky. Thunder rumbled.

"I feel him close by," Luke said. "The bastard thinks his magic is strong enough to hide from me." He laughed. "Hell, his spell isn't *half* as good as Amber's was."

"You let me go," she said, not ever looking away from Cass. "I knew it. You both let me vanish."

"Because you were in pain," Leo mumbled, yanking a hand over his face. "I always hated your pain. Being near us—*it made you hurt more.*"

Cass hated her pain, too. "I'll find Gregory. I'm the one who should have ended him. The pain he caused her—it's on me."

"It's not, Cass!" Her eyes widened in horror. "You never did anything to hurt me."

But he'd never done anything to make her life better, either. And he'd failed to keep her safe.

He summoned his scythe. He'd be using it to take Gregory's head.

Luke waved his hands toward him. "Here you go, Reaper. I'll give you a head start..."

Wind whipped around him, and Amber disappeared.

Cass opened his mouth to roar her name, but then the wind died away. He realized Luke had sent him deeper into the woods. And Cass turned his head when he heard the rustle of footsteps.

Then the snap of a twig. *I'll give you a head start.*

A smile curled Cass's lips. Luke had given him new prey.

Gregory was smiling when he broke her neck. Cass would smile when he used his scythe on Gregory. "Guess what, buddy?" Cass called out as he turned, keeping the scythe close. "Death is ready for you."

***

Amber grabbed Luke's shoulders and shook him—as hard as she could. "*Where* did you send him?"

His eyes widened. Thunder boomed.

"Easy, there, Amber," Leo tried to soothe.

She wasn't in the mood to be soothed. She was pretty sure she'd been *dead,* and her night was hellish. "Where is Cass?"

Luke's brows lifted. "He's Death. He's a Reaper…I sent him off to—you know—reap."

"You sent him to Gregory."

Luke flashed her a smile. "I told you that Gregory was trying to use magic to hide from me. Silly vamp. I could feel him out there, so I sent your Reaper to take what was left of his soul." He inclined his head toward her. "You're welcome."

"I'm *not* thanking you!" Amber screamed. She shook him again, just because. Then she jerked away from him. "You and Leo—you both always think you know what's best!"

"We do," they said in unison.

"You know jackshit," she fired back. Her shoulders heaved. She pointed at Luke. "You…you think I don't get that you didn't want me to sacrifice my wings for you?"

His eyes gleamed. "About that…"

"And *you.*" She pointed to Leo. "You think I didn't know how much you blamed Luke for me giving up my wings? But it wasn't his fault. It wasn't *his* choice. It was mine. Hycim had found a way to hurt Luke. Luke was *weak* because of Hycim. Luke needed time to recover, and my wings bought him that time. They were a small price to pay for Luke's life."

He'd stiffened. "They weren't small to me. They were your *power.*"

"There's more to life than power. You both need to learn that lesson. Maybe then you can avoid killing each other." She rubbed her neck. It still ached. And her back itched. And she felt…weird inside. Shaky.

And scared. So scared…for Cass. "Gregory was the one who gave Hycim all the intel on you—on you both." Her gaze swung between them. "He admitted that he was the one who turned Hycim into a hybrid. Gregory has been gunning for your power all along, Luke, and you didn't *know* that."

His face hardened. "Then it's fitting that the Reaper is about to take his head."

"You sent Cass to do your dirty work before! Gregory was family to him! *Family!* Having Cass take his head…that would be like—like—"

"Like me killing Luke," Leo announced flatly.

Silence.

"Gregory isn't his family," Luke said. "Gregory is one of the fucking vampires who *killed* his family. Then they took in Cass, thinking they could brainwash him into being their attack dog."

At his words, horror flooded her. "You…you knew that all along? And you left Cass with him?" She stared at him in shock. "They cut off his hands! His *hands!*"

"And if Gregory was the one yanking Hycim's strings…then he's also the one responsible for cutting off *your* wings," Luke fired back. "So let your Reaper lover take his vengeance. Let Cass do his worst." He gave a grim shake of his head. "I'm supposed to govern the dark ones, but I don't control them completely. They have their own thoughts. They get fucking out of control, and I do my best to clean up the messes they leave behind. When the vampires took Cass—back when he was a kid—I was dealing with fucking twenty other world-ending problems. The apocalypse is always a step away."

"Amen," Leo mumbled.

"By the time I realized what had happened…Cass was an adult. And he was a killer." Luke huffed out a breath. "I didn't know if I should put him down right away or give the bastard a fighting chance."

The twisting in her stomach got worse. "You won't put him down."

Leo took her arm. "Forget him, okay? You're what matters, not him, not—"

She turned her head and glared at her brother. "Cass matters to me." Her voice was low and lethal.

Leo blinked.

Her head turned back toward Luke. "Send me to him."

"Amber..."

"Send me to him! This fucked-up family reunion can wait! Send me to Cass right now. Right the hell now or I swear I will– "

Luke sighed and waved his hand. "You didn't even ask why I wanted to see you so badly."

He sounded...disappointed.

"I don't care why! I want Cass, I want–"

The wind whipped up around her–and Luke and Leo vanished.

CHAPTER FIFTEEN

Cass faced Gregory, staring at the man who'd first been like a father to him…then a friend.

And now…

An enemy.

"It isn't too late," Gregory said, smiling at him.

Gregory smiled while he broke her neck.

"You and I…we can team up. It is always what I wanted for us. Together, we can take out Luke *and* Leo. We'll be the new order. Everyone else will bow down to us."

"I never wanted anyone to bow to me."

Gregory held up his hands. Hands that were covered with Cass's gloves. "But you want to touch people, don't you? You wanted to touch *her.* Once we have all the power, I can make sure you find someone else to mate, maybe even someone who can bear your touch."

I don't want anyone else. "Amber isn't dead. Luke and Leo brought her back."

Surprise flashed on Gregory's face.

"After I kill you," Cass added, "I'll be taking my gloves back." He smiled. "And then I'll touch her as often as I want."

"If they *did* bring her back, then Luke and Leo want her very badly. They probably have already taken her away from here. You won't see her again. You'll *never* have her again. Not unless you team up with me." His gloved hands slipped behind his body.

"Are you going for your knives?" Cass asked him, tilting his head. "Because I remember…you always kept two knives on you."

Gregory lifted his hands. Each glove held a knife.

Cass stared at those blades.

"Do you remember…" Gregory murmured. "What it was like to lose your hands?"

"I won't be losing my hands tonight. You'll be losing your head."

Gregory seemed to consider that. Then he said, "Your parents didn't think they'd lose their hands, either. But they did. I took your father's hands first. Then your mother's. They were pretty much helpless then. So I drained them. Their blood was very, very powerful. And oddly sweet."

Cass blinked, then he shook his head. No, no, that wasn't—

Gregory struck. He raced forward with a burst of supernatural speed and his knives flashed out, slicing through skin and bone, slicing to take off Cass's wrist.

But Cass twisted up the scythe, and it cut right across Gregory's chest, sending blood flying.

Gregory screamed and stumbled back.

"You…killed my parents?" Cass asked. The world seemed red. Not just from Gregory's blood…but from fury.

Gregory looked down at his chest, then back up at Cass. Anger twisted his face. "Your parents…your relatives…I killed *every* Reaper I could find. I took their power. I *needed* that power. I told you, I had to be strong enough to defeat Luke."

A dull roar filled Cass's ears. He didn't realize he was the one making that animalistic sound, not at first. Pain had clawed up through him, ripping him wide open.

I lived with his clan. All those years…I was with the murderers…

"I wanted to kill you all," Gregory spat. "But you wouldn't die. My vamps chopped off your hands…we drained you…but you came back. You kept coming *back.* So I knew that if I couldn't end you, then I could at least use you."

And he had…for fucking *years.*

"Guess what…?" Gregory whispered. "My vampires? They're here. They're closing in."

Four vampires raced from the dark—and they put themselves between Gregory and Cass.

They bared their fangs.

"Took you fucking long enough," Gregory shouted at them. *"He made me bleed."*

"I'll do a whole lot more than that," Cass promised.

The vampires were a solid wall between him and Gregory. They were a wall that would be coming down.

"It will be just like the old times," Gregory taunted. "We'll take your hands and then drain you dry. When you wake up, we'll do it all over again—"

Wind whipped against Cass's back, but he didn't look over his shoulder. He was too busy lunging toward the four vamps who thought to protect Gregory. The scythe whistled as he brought it down in an arc.

Two vampires fell, minus their heads.

A third yanked out a sharp blade, going for Cass's hand—

Cass touched that vamp. He fell.

Then there was just one vampire between him and Gregory. Just one. "Do you really want to die for him?" Cass asked.

The vampire hesitated. Fear lurked in the darkness of his eyes.

"Were you there?" Cass demanded of that vamp. "When my family died?" Because he knew this vampire—just as he'd known the others.

The two vampires he'd killed with the scythe had been Reginald and Vince. They'd always enjoyed giving their victims too much pain. The third vampire had been McIntosh, an Irish vamp who'd seemed to keep to himself. And the vamp before him—*Stevenson.*

"I was," Stevenson admitted starkly. He squared his shoulders. Lunged for Cass—

The scythe whistled again.

Stevenson's body hit the ground. So did his head.

"Do you *see* him now?" Gregory called out. But he wasn't looking at Cass. He was staring just beyond Cass's shoulder. "See what he is? What *I* made him? You'll remember this, won't you? Even after I'm gone? You'll remember that your lover is a vicious killer."

A rustle sounded behind him. The faintest scent of honey and champagne reached Cass. His heart stopped.

Amber.

"He was born to kill. Crafted to destroy—I *made* him," Gregory boasted.

The rustle came closer and then Amber—she was curling her hand around the scythe that Cass still gripped. "You don't want to do this," she whispered.

Cass turned and stared into her eyes. "There is very little I want more." *You. I want you more…will you turn from me when I take his head?*

She smiled at him—a beautiful, but heart-breaking smile.

And then Amber yanked the scythe away from him. She moved fast—almost a blur—and she struck.

Gregory was dead in an instant. Even a vampire as powerful as Gregory had been could not survive without a head.

"I loved my wings," she said as she stood over his body. "I love my brothers…and you tried to destroy them." She let the scythe fall to the ground near Gregory's body. "And I love Cass…so he will *not* be carrying the weight of your death on his shoulders. And you will never hurt *anyone* I love again."

I love Cass.

Had she really just said that?

Amber turned back toward him. She stared at Cass. He tried to figure out what in the hell to say to her.

"You lived with him for so long…I didn't want you to have his death on your hands."

He looked down at his hands. Hands that couldn't touch her.

"Oh, yeah, right." She bent and yanked the gloves off Gregory. Then she hurried back to Cass and offered him the gloves.

He slipped them on, not looking away from her beautiful face.

"The stories have always said that Luke and Leo will battle one day—battle to the death. They've put off that fight, though they could have clashed years ago." Her voice lowered. "Want to know their secret? Want to know why they don't just end things?"

He didn't really care about Luke and Leo. They could fuck off.

I love Cass. He wanted to talk to her a whole lot more about *that.*

"They haven't fought because neither of them want to carry that guilt. It's different when you kill family. When it's like cutting out your own heart as you make that kill." Her hand lifted and touched his cheek. "And the little boy inside of you…I was afraid he'd still see Gregory as family."

He didn't. Gregory had *killed* his family. "I just see betrayal." His whole life. His whole freaking life had been a lie. "I see pain."

Her lips trembled. "I want to help you see something more."

When he looked at her, he *did* see more. He saw everything. His head bent toward her.

And the earth literally shook.

Lightning crashed. Wind whipped against his body and—

Luke appeared. Luke...and Leo. Luke stood to the right of Amber. Leo was to her left.

"Are you *seriously* trying to kiss here in the middle of all these bodies?" Luke demanded. "Because that is both wrong and sad."

Cass glared at him.

"He *is* the Reaper," Leo put in. "Maybe death is some kind of aphrodisiac for him." He placed his hand on Amber's shoulder. "Yet another reason why you need to stay far away from the guy."

The hell she did.

But Leo's eyes were considering as he stared at Cass. "What did it feel like..." Leo asked quietly. "To kill someone who'd been like family?"

Cass glared at him—and Luke. As if he were the only one with a fucked-up family—the terror twins could hardly judge him. "I wouldn't know."

Leo frowned.

"*I* killed him," Amber said. "With Cass's scythe."

Luke stiffened. "We're done here." He pulled Amber closer and lifted her into his arms. "Good job, Reaper. You held up your end of the deal." His wings flapped. "So I won't be gunning for you."

Amber was struggling to get out of her brother's arms.

"Let her go," Cass barked.

"No." Luke shot into the air, hovering just out of reach, Amber still tight in his embrace. "I wanted to find her for a reason. That reason still stands."

"*Cass!*" Amber yelled.

"She isn't for you," Leo said.

You aren't good enough for her. He knew exactly what the bastard meant.

"Until we meet again, Reaper," Luke called.

Until they—fuck, no! *"Amber!"*

But it was too late. Luke had flown away into the night, taking Amber with him. Taking the one person who fucking *mattered.* Cass started running after them. He shot through the trees, ran down the highway, rushed and rushed and—

I can't see them.

Leo appeared in front of him—his dark and scaly wings stretching behind his body. "Pity you don't have wings of your own," he murmured.

Cass was so fucking *not* in the mood for any more shit. He pulled back his gloved hand and slammed it into the side of Leo's jaw. Leo's head whipped to the right and then he went crashing to the ground.

"*You've* got wings," Cass blasted right back at him. "Take me to her."

Leo rubbed his jaw. He seemed stunned that Cass had been able to hurt him. Leo's brows rose as he stared up at Cass. "You're stronger than I realized."

"Take me to her." Pain clawed at him.

I love Cass. She loved him and he wasn't letting her go.

"Are you stronger than me?" Leo rose to his feet and stared at Cass with something close to wonder in his eyes. "Stronger than Luke? I mean, I didn't believe the stories but I think…you may be able to kill us!"

Cass grabbed the crazy jerk's shoulders and hauled him close. "Don't test me."

But Leo laughed. "I see it—you want her, don't you? Death needs Amber…She's good and she's bad and you're obsessed with her."

"I'm not obsessed. I *love* her."

That stopped Leo's laughter. Cass could practically see the wheels spinning in the guy's mind.

"You're strong," Leo mused. "Strong enough to protect her…"

"Always." He would never let her down again.

"Strong enough to take her from Luke…?"

"Let's find out. Use those damn wings of yours and *get us to them.*" Then he realized he had a bargaining chip. Cass still had that fucking Blade of Truth. He'd strapped it to his ankle—hell, he didn't even remember when he'd done that. But he bent and yanked that knife from the sheath. Amber's bracelet tumbled to the ground when he pulled out the knife. *I remember grabbing that for her, hiding it…wanting to give it back to her.*

"What do you have there?" Leo's voice was cautious.

Cass tucked Amber's bracelet—the bracelet that Luke had given him to start the hunt—into his pocket. He lifted the knife toward Leo. "The Blade of Truth. Figure it has to be worth something, right? Take me to Amber, and it's yours."

Leo's eyes gleamed. "Give me the knife first."

Fuck, he *had* to trust him, but… "Betray me, and you'll feel the scythe take your throat."

"Doubt it. I don't think you would want to hurt Amber. And killing her brother…it *would* hurt her." He took the knife, and it vanished instantly. Then Leo stared at him with a hooded gaze. "Even with the knife, you'll still owe me." Leo gazed straight in Cass's eyes. "If you remember…I have a certain angel who is missing. I may need to call in your services regarding that particular situation."

"Get me to Amber, and yes, I will fucking *owe* you."

Leo grabbed him. "Done."

They flew into the air.

CHAPTER SIXTEEN

"Luke, you bastard, let me go *now!*" Amber screamed.

And...he did.

They dropped to the ground. She stumbled a few feet back from him and realized they were at his island. They'd flown for what felt like for-freaking-ever, and now she saw why—the guy had taken her all the way down to the Florida Keys. They were on the balcony at his house.

"I'm not going to hurt you." Luke had his hands behind his back. "Just...give me a minute, would you?"

She would give him—

A woman walked out onto the balcony. A woman with dark hair and sky blue eyes. A woman who was holding a very, very large black box.

"Mina, my love," Luke called as he held out his hand to her. "Your timing is perfect."

Mina gave a light, oddly musical laugh. "Well, I did see you fly in, so I figured that was my cue." She pressed a kiss to Luke's cheek as he took the box from her. Then Mina's stare slid to Amber. She looked curious and nervous. "Hi," Mina said, tucking a lock of her hair behind her ear. "Luke's...he's told me about you."

Amber's gaze swept over the other woman. "You're the one mated to him."

Mina laughed again—this time, the sound was more nervous than musical. "I'm the one in love with him."

So that story was true. "Does he love you?"

"*He* does," Luke answered. He moved to stand in front of Mina, the box still gripped in his hands. It was a massive box—easily two feet wide and three feet long. "Though I have to confess—after you left, after you lost your wings *for* me—I didn't think I'd ever be able to love anyone." His shoulders sagged a bit. This was the Luke she remembered—the Luke that she'd often felt as if only she knew. *The real man.* "I loved you, and I hurt you. I only seemed to hurt the people I care about."

"I *chose* to give up my wings."

"Right. But you did that for *me.*" He pushed the box at her. "And I can finally give them back to you."

"What?" Her jaw dropped.

"Take the box."

She took the box. Yanked it open. And her knees almost gave way. Her wings were in that box. Shimmering, silken...as soft as a dream. As perfect as her memory.

Amber felt tears on her cheeks.

"I can't...I can't put them back on you." Now Luke's voice was ragged. "Because the fairy part of you? That's the part I could never touch."

Her supposed good side.

Luke and Leo were two distinct halves. Luke had gotten the dark powers. Leo had been given the light ones. But she was different from her brothers. Light and dark had merged within her, always fighting.

Nearly breaking her apart.

"I can get Leo to do it," Luke continued gruffly. "I'll force Leo to—"

Wind whipped against her. She couldn't look away from her wings. Her beautiful wings. Still dark and lovely, after all this time.

Magic.

"Force me to do what?" Leo demanded.

Because, of course, he was there.

"My wings," she whispered. "Luke got my wings back."

Stunned silence.

"I can't put them back on her," Luke said quietly. "I don't have that magic. Only you—"

Leo took the wings without another word. He stared into Amber's eyes. "Please don't fucking give them up again."

"Yeah," Luke added, his voice gruff. "You don't want to know what I did to get those back."

Then Leo was behind her. Her head still bowed forward because she couldn't believe it. Her magic—her wings.

She felt the glow in her back. Felt the pain that she'd carried in her scars melt away.

And then…

Power flooded through her, pouring into every single cell in her body. She looked down at her hands and her skin was glowing. She tossed back her head and she laughed—and she *flew*. For the first time in so many years, she—

"You are beautiful."

Cass.

Cass was there. Standing right beside Luke. Staring at her as if she were the most amazing thing that he'd ever seen.

She flew to him. *Always, to him.*

"I have my wings, Cass!" She had her power fully restored. "I'm back! I'm—I'm whole again!"

"You were always whole to me." He smiled at her. "You've always been perfect to me."

She realized he meant those words.

He reached into his pocket and pulled out something small…something gold…something—

Amber gave a quick cry. "My bracelet!" She'd thought it was long gone.

But Cass gently hooked it around her wrist. "It brought me to you. I just…I needed to bring it back to you." Then Cass looked down at his gloved hands. "Guess Luke and I both wanted to return something to you." He glanced at Luke. "That's why you wanted her back, huh, Luke? To give her the wings?"

"Amber had her damn *hide-me* spell in place. I couldn't find her and she deserved those damn wings. I would have made *any* deal to get her back."

His deal. Amber blinked and a little of her joy faded. She looked at Luke. "You promised him…a mate."

Luke gave a grim nod of his head.

"Someone he could touch." She reached for one of Cass's gloved hands. "Someone he wouldn't fear hurting."

"Yes," Luke gritted and it sounded as if he were choking on nails. "And Cass held up his end of the bargain…so that means I will, too. *Dammit.*"

She shook her head and the pain in her chest got worse. Cass deserved to touch—he deserved to be happy. But it was going to tear out her heart—her soul—when he went to another. She loved him, so much. *So fast. So deep. I fell for him…*

"Take off his gloves, Amber," Luke ordered.

"Wh-what?"

"You're the one." Luke crossed his arms over his chest. Mina patted his shoulder, as if to comfort him. "I knew it all fucking along—why do you think those gloves worked?"

She'd feared... "They were made of fairy wings?"

"Dust. Fucking fairy dust...and I can't even believe I just said that shit." He glared at Cass. "The last bit of dust that existed. You know where fairy dust comes from, Reaper? It comes from fairies when they cry. Their tears turn into pure magic. I gave you that magic and when it worked...hell, I *knew* Amber would be the one for you. She was born—fucking literally—to be touched by you."

Amber yanked the gloves off Cass.

"No, wait," Cass said. "What if it doesn't work, what if—"

"Then my brothers can bring my ass back." *Again.* She wrapped her hands around his. And she felt the heat instantly. Warm, consuming...

Binding.

Not killing. A connection was forging right between them that had *nothing* to do with death and everything to do with love.

"I'm touching you," Cass rasped.

She brought their linked hands up. She kissed the back of his hand.

"I'm *touching* you!"

Amber laughed.

And she put his hands right over her heart—the heart that the Reaper owned. "I love you."

His eyes blazed at her. "Amber, you are my world." He pulled her close. Kissed her frantically. "I love you."

Joy pulsed through her again. It had been so long since she felt true joy…so long…she rose, her wings lifting her up easily and Amber made sure Cass flew with her. She knew—Cass would always be with her.

"Amber!" It was Luke, calling out to her.

She glanced down at him.

"Is he really what you want?"

"He's everything I want."

Then Luke nodded, grimly.

She'd be talking to him again—to him and to Leo and trying to figure out how to save them all. Just like in the old days.

But for that moment…she didn't want to be with her brothers. She just wanted to be with the man she loved. The man who'd faced off against Luke. Against Leo.

For her.

Amber flew into the night with Cass.

***

"How long have you been planning that?" Leo asked, tilting his head as he watched Amber fly away.

Luke shrugged. Then he moved closer to his Mina. He reached for her hand. "Perhaps…ever since the day I realized that our sister would need a very powerful protector." He tossed a grim smile at Leo. "Because she's tied to us, she will always have a target on her back."

"And Death can stop that target?"

"He's almost as strong as we are."

"I wonder…" Leo rubbed his chin. "Perhaps he's *stronger*."

Once more, Luke shrugged. "Hopefully, we won't be finding out that answer any time soon."

Mina gave a soft sigh. "You sent him after her because you knew they'd wind up together."

He kissed her cheek. "I will confess that I knew my sister had a dark side…and I suspected Cass would appeal to her."

She laughed. "You're a matchmaker."

No, he was something much darker. He was a man who had to plan for *every* contingency. And when his enemies came for him, he had to make sure that his sister lived.

And…perhaps…he'd wanted her to be happy.

When I was younger, Amber taught me about love. I could see it in her eyes. Now he stared into Mina's eyes…

And he knew love again. A very, very different kind of love.

"You made one mistake," Leo said from behind him. "You didn't count on *me*."

Luke glanced back at him. "Of course, I did. I knew you'd put the wings back for her."

"No, no, I *made* a deal with Cass, too."

Was that supposed to be a big deal? "Good for you." He waved toward the sky. "Now, go fly away. I have plans." He smiled at Mina. "Very important plans."

His brother lingered.

Luke sighed. "Don't you have an angel to find?" He tilted his head to glance at his brother.

And that was when he caught it…the briefest of flashes, but it was there. *Envy*. In Leo's eyes. The great and powerful Lord of the Light envied him.

Because in the end, Leo is alone.

It hadn't always been that way. Once, they'd been so close…until the world had said they must be enemies.

Until Luke had been told he was bad.

And Leo was good.

Only lately, Leo had begun to show more than a few *bad* qualities of his own.

"I do have an angel to find." Leo nodded grimly. "Good-bye." He turned away.

"I think you've got the wrong girl," Luke said, truly considering things now. "You don't need someone so…*good*. Perhaps, brother, what you really need is a walk on the darker side."

Leo glanced back at him. "That side would lead me straight to hell."

"Oh, yes, no doubt." Luke smiled. "But wouldn't it be a fun ride?"

Leo flew away.

Luke laughed.

And he knew just what trouble he would be sending his brother's way.

CHAPTER SEVENTEEN

I can touch her.

Amber stood before Cass, her skin bare, her beautiful wings fluttering behind her back. They were in his home, his sanctuary, in the middle of the North Carolina's Smoky Mountains.

"What are you waiting for?" Amber asked as she stepped toward him.

Part of him was still afraid. He wanted her so much. And if he lost her—

She caught his hand in hers. He felt that surge of warmth again. Their connection. No death.

Life.

And he let go of the fucking fear. He wrapped his arms around her. He pulled her close. His mouth took hers in a ravenous kiss. She met him—going wild. Her nails raked over his skin. Her lips parted beneath his. His tongue swept inside, tasting her, taking…

They tumbled back onto his bed. He had to touch her—everywhere. His fingers trailed over her silken skin. She was so soft. So incredibly soft.

His hand touched her breast. The nipple was tight, pink, and he caught it between his fingertips. He tugged on it, and Amber gave a hot, little moan.

He put his mouth on her other breast. Licked and kissed and sucked as he kept touching her. "Want to touch you forever," he muttered and kissed her nipple again. "Forever."

She laughed. She moaned. She arched up against him.

His hand trailed lower. Over the gentle curve of her stomach. *Every single inch.* He wanted to touch her everywhere.

And he would.

He *could.*

He kissed his way down her stomach, following the path that his hands had taken, and then he was stroking her thighs. She gasped and he knew she liked his touch.

His body trembled. His cock was fully erect and jerking toward her, but he wasn't done. There was so much more to touch.

He pushed her legs apart. Trailed his fingers up her thighs. Then he was touching her core. Sliding his fingers into her, feeling every single flex of her body around him. He withdrew his fingers, then thrust deep.

Her hips surged toward him.

She was wet and she was hot, and she was so tight. He was touching heaven, and he *never* wanted to stop.

He stroked her, moving his fingers faster and deeper. Pressing his thumb to her clit. Pushing the pleasure on her again and again and again.

She came…she came from his touch and Amber grabbed the bedding and fisted it in her hands.

He didn't stop. He kept thrusting his fingers into her. Kept stroking her—her cream was on him, coating his fingers.

My touch isn't just death. It will be pleasure for her. Always, for her.

He licked her breasts. He kissed her. And he kept thrusting his fingers into her, stroking her sex, learning all of her secrets.

Every. Last. One.

She came again, choking out his name.

He wasn't done.

His hand slowly pulled from her body. He licked his fingers…tasting her. Sweet, sweet fucking honey and champagne.

"Cass…" Amber's voice was husky. So sexy.

She reached for him, but he caught her hands. Cass twined their fingers together and then pushed her hands back, on either side of her head. Her legs rose, wrapping around him, and she pressed that hot heaven against him.

He drove into her. Held her hands tightly and thrust as deep as he could go. She was slick from her desire, from her climaxes, and he sank in to the hilt. He withdrew, thrust deep, and couldn't stop. A frenzy took over—a desire so consuming that all he could do was feel.

Thrust.

Take.

Consume.

She came around him, climaxing again as she *shouted* his name this time. He felt the contractions of her sex and he let himself go. Cass pumped into her, driving over and over with hard, heavy thrusts so that the bed slammed into the wall. He emptied into her, and he knew he would *never, ever* get enough of her.

He kissed her again. Kissed her while he was still buried balls-deep in her body.

Then his head lifted. He stared into her eyes.

And he knew…he was about to have her again. His hands slowly released hers. His right hand moved to caress her cheek. *Touching her.*

Her beautiful eyes seemed to warm. She stared at him—not with fear. But with love.

And he understood that he would love her forever, would cherish her forever. Not because she was the only one he could touch.

Because she was the only one who touched *him.* Amber was the only one who'd reached the cold heart he kept inside. She'd taught him to love. She'd shown the Reaper that there was so much more to life than just death.

His lips pressed to hers.

And he was finally at peace.

THE END

###

Don't miss the next book in the Bad Things series, BROKEN ANGEL, available 12/13/2016.

BROKEN ANGEL (BAD THINGS, BOOK 4)

What happens when an angel falls? Find out in Book 4 of Cynthia Eden's "Bad Things" series, BROKEN ANGEL.

Angel Lila is being hunted—she can feel the hunter closing in behind her. Every move she makes, he's stalking after her. But does the werewolf on her trail want to destroy her—or can he protect her from the growing darkness that she is trying so desperately to fight?

Werewolf Rayce Lovel doesn't know what to do with an angel—especially one who makes him think too much about paradise. Lila may be heavenly, but every time he's near her, Rayce wants to sin. Angels aren't supposed to feel, but Lila was introduced to the world by way of pain. Pain is all she's known for far too long, and now, Rayce is tempted to introduce gorgeous Lila to pleasure.

But the longer an angel stays out of heaven, the more dangerous she can become. Lila sinks deeper into the darkness with each night that passes, and she finds herself becoming a pawn in an eternal battle...good versus evil. Is Rayce really her protector? Perhaps he is just the hungry wolf who has been sent to ensure that Lila never sets foot back in her paradise.

A fallen angel has a bad side...and that side is about to be set free.

A NOTE FROM THE AUTHOR

Thank you so much for taking the time to read UNDEAD OR ALIVE. The Reaper was a new character for me, and I had a great time writing about his adventures with Amber. I hope you enjoyed their story! And don't forget…the next "Bad Things" book will be out in December. BROKEN ANGEL is coming soon.

If you'd like to stay updated on my releases and sales, please join my newsletter list www.cynthiaeden.com/newsletter/. You can also check out my Facebook page www.facebook.com/cynthiaedenfanpage. I love to post giveaways over at Facebook!

Again, thank you for reading UNDEAD OR ALIVE.

Best,
Cynthia Eden
www.cynthiaeden.com

ABOUT THE AUTHOR

Award-winning author Cynthia Eden writes dark tales of paranormal romance and romantic suspense. She is a *New York Times, USA Today, Digital Book World,* and *IndieReader* best-seller. Cynthia is also a three-time finalist for the RITA® award. Since she began writing full-time in 2005, Cynthia has written over fifty novels and novellas.

Cynthia is a southern girl who loves horror movies, chocolate, and happy endings. More information about Cynthia and her books may be found at: http://www.cynthiaeden.com or on her Facebook page at: http://www.facebook.com/cynthiaedenfanpage. Cynthia is also on Twitter at http://www.twitter.com/cynthiaeden.

HER WORKS

Paranormal Romance

Bad Things

- The Devil In Disguise (Bad Things, Book 1)
- On The Prowl (Bad Things, Book 2)
- Broken Angel (Bad Things, Book 3) - Available 12/13/2016

Blood and Moonlight Series

- Bite The Dust (Blood and Moonlight, Book 1)
- Better Off Undead (Blood and Moonlight, Book 2)
- Bitter Blood (Blood and Moonlight, Book 3)
- Blood and Moonlight (The Complete Series)

Purgatory Series

- The Wolf Within (Purgatory, Book 1)
- Marked By The Vampire (Purgatory, Book 2)

- Charming The Beast (Purgatory, Book 3)
- Deal with the Devil (Purgatory, Book 4)
- The Beasts Inside (Purgatory, Books 1 to 4)

Bound Series

- Bound By Blood (Bound Book 1)
- Bound In Darkness (Bound Book 2)
- Bound In Sin (Bound Book 3)
- Bound By The Night (Bound Book 4)
- Forever Bound (Bound, Books 1 to 4)
- Bound in Death (Bound Book 5)

Night Watch Series

- Eternal Hunter (Night Watch Book 1)
- I'll Be Slaying You (Night Watch Book 2)
- Eternal Flame (Night Watch Book 3)

Phoenix Fire Series

- Burn For Me (Phoenix Fire, Book 1)
- Once Bitten, Twice Burned (Phoenix Fire, Book 2)
- Playing With Fire (Phoenix Fire, Book 3)

The Fallen Series

- Angel of Darkness (The Fallen Book 1)
- Angel Betrayed (The Fallen Book 2)
- Angel In Chains (The Fallen Book 3)
- Avenging Angel (The Fallen Book 4)

Midnight Trilogy

- Hotter After Midnight (Book One in the Midnight Trilogy)
- Midnight Sins (Book Two in the Midnight Trilogy)
- Midnight's Master (Book Three in the Midnight Trilogy)

Paranormal Anthologies

- A Vampire's Christmas Carol

Loved By Gods Series

- Bleed For Me

ImaJinn

- The Vampire's Kiss
- The Wizard's Spell

Other Paranormal

- Immortal Danger
- Never Cry Wolf
- A Bit of Bite

Romantic Suspense

Killer Instinct

- After The Dark (Killer Instinct, Book 1) - Available 03/28/2017

LOST Series

- Broken (LOST, Book 1)
- Twisted (LOST, Book 2)

- Shattered (LOST, Book 3)
- Torn (LOST, Book 4)
- Taken (LOST, Book 5) - Available 11/29/2016

Dark Obsession Series

- Watch Me (Dark Obsession, Book 1)
- Want Me (Dark Obsession, Book 2)
- Need Me (Dark Obsession, Book 3)
- Beware Of Me (Dark Obsession, Book 4)
- Only For Me (Dark Obsession, Books 1 to 4)

Mine Series

- Mine To Take (Mine, Book 1)
- Mine To Keep (Mine, Book 2)
- Mine To Hold (Mine, Book 3)
- Mine To Crave (Mine, Book 4)
- Mine To Have (Mine, Book 5)
- Mine To Protect (Mine, Book 6)

Montlake - For Me Series

- Die For Me (For Me, Book 1)
- Fear For Me (For Me, Book 2)
- Scream For Me (For Me, Book 3)

Harlequin Intrigue - The Battling McGuire Boys

- Confessions (Battling McGuire Boys…Book 1)
- Secrets (Battling McGuire Boys…Book 2)

- Suspicions (Battling McGuire Boys…Book 3)
- Reckonings (Battling McGuire Boys…Book 4)
- Deceptions (Battling McGuire Boys…Book 5)
- Allegiances (Battling McGuire Boys…Book 6)

Harlequin Intrigue - Shadow Agents Series

- Alpha One (Shadow Agents, Book 1)
- Guardian Ranger (Shadow Agents, Book 2)
- Sharpshooter (Shadow Agents, Book 3)
- Glitter And Gunfire (Shadow Agents, Book 4)
- Undercover Captor (Shadow Agents, Book 5)
- The Girl Next Door (Shadow Agents, Book 6)
- Evidence of Passion (Shadow Agents, Book 7)
- Way of the Shadows (Shadow Agents, Book 8)

Deadly Series

- Deadly Fear (Book One of the Deadly Series)
- Deadly Heat (Book Two of the Deadly Series)

- Deadly Lies (Book Three of the Deadly Series)

Contemporary Anthologies

- First Taste of Darkness
- Sinful Secrets

Other Romantic Suspense

- Until Death
- Femme Fatale
- Christmas With A Spy

Young Adult Paranormal

- The Better To Bite (A Young Adult Paranormal Romance)

Anthologies

Contemporary Anthologies

- "All I Want for Christmas" in The Naughty List

Paranormal Anthologies

- "New Year's Bites" in A Red Hot New Year
- "Wicked Ways" in When He Was Bad
- "Spellbound" in Everlasting Bad Boys
- "In the Dark" in Belong to the Night
- Howl For It

Made in the USA
Lexington, KY
25 February 2019